MAKE ME

MEN OF GOLD MOUNTAIN

REBECCA
BROOKS

Entangled Publishing, LLC
2614 South Timberline Road
Suite 109
Fort Collins, CO 80525
Visit our website at www.entangledpublishing.com.

Brazen is an imprint of Entangled Publishing, LLC. For more information on our titles, visit www.brazenbooks.com.

Edited by Alycia Tornetta
Cover design by Cover Couture
Cover art from Shutterstock

Manufactured in the United States of America

First Edition October 2016

ENTANGLED
BRAZEN

Dear Reader,

I am so happy to introduce you to *Make Me Stay*, the first novel in the Men of Gold Mountain Series and my first book to come out with Entangled Brazen. This story is especially close to my heart. It combines a place I love, the Pacific Northwest, with one of my favorite sports, skiing. It celebrates family, commitment, and what it means to do what's right — even, or especially, when what's right involves hard choices and compromise.

I grew up in Massachusetts. Every winter, I was lucky to spend my school vacations skiing with my family, just as Sam does. (Although the similarities end there. My family doesn't own a billion-dollar company. Alas.) I still ski with my dad, and it's something I look forward to every year.

One time, my dad and I were at Mt. Sunapee in New Hampshire and noticed the most graceful skier either of us had ever seen. Rather than carrying poles, as skiers normally do, he was lifting his arms as though flying. We realized he was coaching a high school girl's racing team and we followed them for a few runs. I had raced for a year and a half in high school, until an injury sidelined me. This coach made being on the team look a lot more fun than I remembered!

Years later, that moment became the kernel for *Make Me Stay*. Sam sees Austin leading his team down the slopes and can't turn away from him. She can't turn away even when it means risking everything that's important to her: her career, her company, her father's legacy.

The setting of Gold Mountain is based on a hiking trip my husband and I took to the tiny town of Glacier, WA. Wow, is it beautiful there! I knew I had to set my ski novel in the Cascades, and that one book wouldn't be enough. That's when the Men of Gold Mountain series was born: four books to follow four friends through the seasons. I'm excited to introduce you to Austin and Sam and to the home they make together in Gold Mountain, WA. Though this is the winter novel, you won't have to bundle up with chemistry this hot!

Don't miss signing up for my newsletter at http://rebeccabrooksromance.com to see pictures from the Cascades and more on what inspires me. You can also find me on Twitter, Facebook, and Instagram to keep up with where I'm traveling now.

With love,

Rebecca

For Robert, always.
And for my father and grandfather, who taught me to ski.

Chapter One

Sam zipped her jacket tight around her neck and lifted her goggles. The world shocked to brightness, blue sky, and the bone white of snow. She'd expected to change her mind at the last minute and head to the office instead. But here she was, cold on her cheeks like a kiss and a slap all at once.

She'd almost been afraid her car would drive to the skyscraper no matter what, as though the wheels couldn't turn anywhere else. But somewhere between her second and third caffeine injection of the day, she'd put the mug down, met her reflection in the wall of windows looking out at Puget Sound, and said—literally, out loud, like her mother, who'd started muttering to herself now that she was alone—"Get it together, Kane."

She'd been in her pajamas and holding a throw pillow, so not exactly in what her colleagues called "wolf mode" when they thought she couldn't hear. But the words came out low, edged with a growl, the signature tone she used when it was time to stop *shilly-shallying*—her father's phrase—and *get shit done*. That was her preferred way of saying it, even if she could still hear him admonishing her not to curse.

It was three years to the day since they'd buried her father, and although Sam continued to hear his voice in her head, she was tired. Tired of all the hours in the office, tired of working nonstop to take over his role, tired of the weight of her grief.

But all she had left was one task. Once she convinced the last owner to sell, the land purchase would finally be ready to go. Bill Kane's legacy was going to happen. Gold Mountain was going to be *the* destination for Seattleites year-round.

Gold Mountain was going to prove that Samantha Kane could do it—and then some.

As long as she could get that holdout, a man named Austin Reede, to stop ruining her plans.

Sam wasn't even asking for all his land. It was only half his acreage. He wouldn't have to move, and they'd keep a line of trees in place so he'd barely see the new condos from his yard. He should have been thrilled to keep all that *and* get a handsome check in the process.

But according to her assistant, Mr. Reede had stopped taking their calls. When Sam tried him herself, she reached only voicemail. Adjusting the expansion to work around his property wasn't an option. Sam couldn't appear weak to her board.

Which was why she'd decided not to go to her office today. It was time to stop sending letters and lawyers and start handling Mr. Reede herself. She'd offer more money, a ski run named after him, a condo for himself…whatever he wanted, as long as he signed.

She'd stopped by his house, but there was no car out front. He was probably at work. She knew from his file that he was on ski patrol and a racing coach—neither of which could pay very well. Another reason he should be jumping on this deal.

Fortunately, Sam was prepared to wait. In fact, she'd been counting on it.

She didn't bother wasting time checking into the hotel. She parked at the mountain and locked her laptop, blueprints, and files in the trunk. Soon she was riding the chairlift, breathing the clean mountain air. Knowing she couldn't access everything immediately even if she wanted to gave her a lightness she didn't know she possessed, despite the skis, boots, and heavy jacket weighing her down.

Not that she was entirely free. A vibration buzzed in her pocket—no doubt someone from the office who didn't know what "unavailable" meant. She used her teeth to yank off her mitten and pulled out the phone.

The name on the caller ID made her groan. She knew she shouldn't answer even as she did.

"I can't talk," she said with her mouth full of mitten.

"Samantha? Is that you?" She could picture Jim eyeing the phone to check that it was really her name lit up on the screen, his nose wrinkling in that face he made whenever something didn't go according to plan.

Which of course happened all the time. He walked around the boardroom as though the chairs permanently smelled.

Sam pulled the mitten out of her mouth and gripped it tightly. "I can't talk," she repeated.

"What the hell is going on?"

"Is this about work?"

"No, Samantha. This is about the voicemail you left me at six o'clock this morning."

"If it's not about work then I can't talk." She paused. "And even if it is about work, I still can't talk."

"What are you doing? What's that noise? Samantha, where are you?"

She wedged the phone up under her helmet so it was secure against her ear and tugged the mitten back on her hand before it froze.

"I have to go," she said.

He switched tracks, his voice dripping into that "I am not an asshole" register he used with clients right after he'd just been an asshole. "Samantha," he soothed, "I know we've had our ups and downs, but we have to talk about this. You can't leave me a message like that and then vanish."

Sam's eyes widened as the top of the mountain surged closer. She was running out of time.

"No, seriously, Jim, I have to get off the phone. I'm about to—"

The guy next to her nudged her shoulder. "Look, lady, are you planning to ride this thing back down or what?"

Sam swung her feet off the bar and lifted it overhead. Too soon the ground zoomed up and the chair banked down and then she was standing, the back of the chair hitting her calves and nudging her forward. *Just like riding a bike*, she reminded herself as she glided down the embankment, the phone still lodged by her ear.

Jim's baritone droned on. "Samantha, what are you doing? Are you going to be at the office later? I'll take you to lunch and we can talk this through like adults."

"I'm not at the office. And no, you can't take me to lunch, today or any other day."

"What the hell has gotten into you?"

Not you, anymore, she thought wryly as she skated away from the top of the lift. But that definitely wasn't on the script she'd practiced for herself in the car. "Listen, Jim. I know this may come as a surprise, but I trust we can both handle this as professionals. We have a long history of working together, and I value your contributions."

It came out less gracefully than it had in her head. *Condescending. The word you're looking for is "condescending."* But she plowed on. "I mean it this time. We really are done."

"'I value your contributions'?" Jim snorted over the

phone. "Come to the office, Samantha. Let's at least do lunch."

But Sam wasn't going to let him wear her down this time. "There's nothing more to talk about. I'm hanging up now."

"Stop!" he demanded. "You can't just—"

"I'm your boss, Jim," she interrupted.

She heard the air hissing out from between his teeth. "I see how it is. You tell me that won't be a problem, until you conveniently decide to pull rank."

Sam stood up straighter. "Let's not make this personal. I'd like you to get Marie and Cody to run the numbers again before the two o'clock. Loop me in on the minutes, we have to be ready with our strategy the second the purchase goes through. And Jim?" She didn't wait for him to answer. "I'll arrange for someone to drop your clothes back at your place. Don't worry about a thing."

She hung up before he could get another word in.

The wolf. That was what they called her, and she knew that was what he was thinking right now. *Cold-ass bitch.* They loved it when she brought in the clients and made the money flow. They hated her for it, too.

Except for Jim Rutherford. Because he always had the best. The best suits, the best wine, the best women. It made hot tears smart behind her eyes to think of how she'd let him parade her around, the head Kane of Kane Enterprises on his arm. Her past four attempts to break up with him hadn't worked. He'd kept calling, sending flowers, showing up to take her out as though they hadn't had the conversation at all.

But not this time. Sam called her assistant, Steven, about Jim's clothes, knowing he'd be discreet, and reminded him to stay alert to anything he heard from the board about her performance. She hadn't exactly cleared this little stunt she was pulling. If she showed up at the office tomorrow with Mr. Reede's signature, they'd laud her. If they thought she'd run off for a vacation in the middle of their busiest time, the response wouldn't quite be the same.

Well, what they didn't know couldn't hurt them. She turned her phone to silent and tucked it away. Other people got to take breaks. Even her father had put everything on hold so he could take his daughter skiing as soon as the first snow fell. He was well established by then, but still. Why couldn't she have a few hours, too?

Samantha Kane, CEO of Kane Enterprises, recently dubbed one of *Fortune's* Most Powerful Women and a perennial favorite in their 40 Under 40 lists. The leading real estate developer in the rapidly growing Pacific Northwest. Samantha Kane, the wolf, the bitch.

In such desperate need of a break.

Sam looked out at the view—snow-peaked mountains dipping into valleys thick with trees. There was a cluster of buildings around the base of the mountain and then a whole lot of nothing as far as the eye could see.

Soon, she thought with a thrill, *that's all going to change*.

• • •

Austin always laid first tracks in the morning. He got up with the dawn, fed Chloe, and then took her for a run. When they came back from the trails in the woods behind his house, both of them panting as they chased each other through the snow, he threw on his gear. It didn't matter the weather, or how busy the day, or whether or not his knee ached. He didn't let anything stop him.

Especially not his memories. They came in flashes, worst in the floating hours as he drifted out of sleep. His father, red-faced, screaming not to leave. How his mother's suitcase dropped with a thud. He saw, always, in the back of his mind, the glint of metal under the wan yellow of the garage light. A hammer coming down. And then a cry—his own? His mother's? — and nothing but pain.

Austin got up every day to ski because that was how he got up at all. It was the only way to push back against the attack that had effectively ended his family, his career, and almost ended him.

But it hadn't.

So, in the mornings, he shot down the steep face of Diamond Bowl, or turned in the deep powder in the trees if they'd been blasted with snow the night before. His lift ticket was a perk of his job as a ski coach at Gold Mountain Academy, and it let him on the mountain before anyone else lined up for the day. Some days he took the lift as high as it would go and climbed the rest of the way to the peak until the only sound was his panting and the brush of his poles in new snow. He'd pause at the top, listening to the wind sweeping clear above the tree line. Then he'd tip over the edge and shoot down.

He skied in the snow, in the rain, in clouds so thick it was only because he knew the mountain like he knew his own skin that he had any idea where to turn. But he lived for mornings like this, when the sky was so clear and the sun so bright he knew why they called it Gold Mountain, because from up top the whole thing shone.

It was worth a fortune, this land. Hell, the number of zeros on the check Kane Enterprises wanted to write him made his head spin. But every inch of it meant more than money to him. It was where he'd found himself, where he'd come back from the edge of injury and despair, where he'd been reminded of his body and what it could do. It was his home, and he wasn't giving it up — no matter how hard Samantha Kane tried.

Wind pierced through him as he bombed down the slope. They'd called him the cleanest skier the Olympic team had ever seen, so precise he could repeat the exact same line down a course over and over again. Looking up at his tracks, he wondered, not for the first time, what he was going to do when everything he loved about this place was taken away.

Austin wasn't naive. He knew the Henderson family, which owned the ski resort, was eager to get out of debt. And the owners of the additional land Kane Enterprises was purchasing were happy enough with their offers. He didn't blame anyone for wanting to sell.

But that didn't mean he wanted a company in Seattle that made its fortune in logging a generation ago to take over. Some people said after Bill Kane died that the deal wouldn't go through, but then there came word that his daughter, Samantha, was determined to make the development even greater than originally planned. Like the more trees she ordered chopped, the more her father's legacy would grow.

They'd upped their offer by 25 percent, then 50, then more, like they didn't understand that when Austin said no, he meant it. He wasn't selling half his property to those bastards so they could turn the woods behind his home into soulless condominiums for the rich weekend crowd. Where would Chloe run? Where would he look out and know he'd finally found a place to call home?

No one is taking anything, he reminded himself as he made the last turns down to the base of the mountain. They couldn't force him to sell.

But when he came home, he had a voicemail. Steven Park, the message said, and his stomach tightened. He'd never spoken with Samantha Kane directly, but he knew her assistant better than he wanted to. You don't forget someone you've hung up on more than once.

"Ms. Kane will be coming to Gold Mountain to meet with you in person," the message said. "I'm sure I don't need to remind you that she is *very* busy and is taking time out of her schedule to personally address your concerns. Please let us know when we can—"

Austin pressed delete. He must have really ticked off the boss lady if she was deigning to make the trip all the way up here herself.

Good. Let them try to intimidate him. It would be even more satisfying to tell her off to her face than it was to rip up her company's letters and shove them in the recycling bin.

Three days a week Austin worked on the ski patrol team before practice, but today was an off day, so he hit the gym in his basement and planned his lessons for the week. He did plyometric jumps and balance holds until his muscles were shaking and he'd purged all thoughts of Kane Enterprises from his mind. Then he showered and ate as he went over the videos from last week's race.

Amelia, his top skier, had won by a huge margin. Anyone scanning the times would be thrilled. Amelia Derringer was the best Gold Mountain had ever seen. For the first time in the school's history, there was an opportunity for a kid from Gold Mountain Academy to race in Park City, Utah, and try for the U.S. Ski Team.

But to the trained eye, Amelia's recent victory was a careless win, the seconds between her and silver fewer than they should have been. He'd been going easy on her. That was going to have to change.

Chloe came up to rest her head in his lap, and he rubbed the soft tips of her ears between his finger and thumb. He felt bad when it was time to rouse her to load up the truck.

"I'll be back soon, baby doll," he promised. "You can come, but it's cold out there."

She poked her nose out the door, but he'd tired her out on their run and she retreated back into the house.

"That's what I figured. If that Kane lady comes poking around, don't forget to growl. Amelia can do it," he added as he grabbed his keys. "She's done that same run two seconds faster, and that was on a practice day."

Chloe cocked her head, confused as to why Austin was still standing in the doorway. *I'm really losing it.* So alone he was talking strategy with his dog, trying to figure out the magic words to say to Amelia to remind her she knew how to win.

No one had ever told him that in his own life. But it didn't matter that he'd missed his chances. He wasn't the kind of person who backed down anymore. He wouldn't let the kids on his team accept defeat.

And he wouldn't show a hint of weakness to that damned Samantha Kane.

Chapter Two

Sam coasted down the slopes, getting used to skiing again. Getting used to skiing without her dad.

Surprisingly, she was having a good time. She knew he wouldn't have wanted her to stay away from the mountain. He would have insisted she keep going without him, even though they'd always skied together.

The day kept getting better as her confidence on the slopes returned. But every trip up the chairlift took her by a giant clock at the base of the mountain, reminding her she was no closer to sitting down with Mr. Reede.

This is the last run, she resolved as she squinted up at the afternoon sun. *You've had your fun. Now it's time to go in.*

She hopped on the lift, and that was when she spotted the man skiing down.

Sam had watched plenty of good skiers—her dad was one of them. But she'd never seen anyone ski like the guy coming down the trail. His turns were so fluid it was more like skating, big round S's making a clean line all the way down.

But it wasn't just the turns. It was the gracefulness, the

confidence, an essential *now-ness* in the way his body moved. She couldn't figure out what he was doing on a normal run with normal people like her until she saw the trail of skiers snaking behind him, mimicking his turns. The five girls had Gold Mountain Race Club stitched in gold lettering on their matching blue jackets.

When Sam got to the top of the lift, she turned down the same run where she'd seen him, as though she could soak up some of his skill through osmosis alone. She wasn't sure she'd catch them, but she was in luck. They were clustered on the top of a knoll, the girls standing in a horseshoe while the man demonstrated something in the middle. She stopped above them, pretending to take a break on the run as she tried to listen in.

Like the girls, the coach wore racing skins with a bright spiderweb design. He had a fitted fleece vest over the top, partially unzipped. Sweat dampened his chest. He was wearing a helmet and goggles so she couldn't see his face, but she could say with certainty that the scruff along his jawline worked plenty well. That, along with the fact that every muscle in his thighs showed through the racing skins, made her slide shamelessly closer to where the group stood.

Not that she was seriously on the market. But she could look, couldn't she? Out of the office, out on the prowl, and—for a few hours at least—just a regular red-blooded woman enjoying her day.

She was surprised when the coach held out his hands and gathered the poles from the girls. He stuck them on the side of the trail and motioned for them to watch. Sam had no idea what he was doing—what racer didn't use poles? But then he began to ski.

His body crouched low as he crossed the trail. As his weight shifted and he began to rotate, everything lifted. His arms, unencumbered by the poles, rose like wings. He brought his hands fluidly overhead and then settled down into a tuck, only to spring up again around the next curve. He made it look effortless, as though he were floating, his whole body heaving a sigh. It was something Sam had never seen or thought about before, not just good skiing but *beautiful* skiing, a strong, graceful dance across the snow.

The man came to a stop and watched the girls as one by one they tried to imitate his movements. They were awkward, still learning flight, but Sam could see how the exercise forced them to reconsider their weight, their relationship to their skis and their own bodies. They were lighter, somehow. More connected to the snow. The team gathered around the coach, and he set off again. This time, they followed directly in his tracks. They snaked down the run in a long line, a single organism turning and rising at the same time.

Sam latched on to the end, following along. She still had her poles, and she didn't want to draw attention to herself by raising her arms overhead, but she let her legs come up and her breath fill her with each turn. The timing was different than what she was used to. She felt herself shift into the next arc before she'd finished the last, so that she never really ended a turn but flowed into the next. It was such a simple shift and yet it changed everything. When she veered away from them at the bottom of the trail she felt like laughing, her whole body buoyant and filled with light.

There was no way she could go inside now. She had to practice that new shift to her weight, the swell of the turns. She'd already taken the day off anyway. Surely a few more hours wouldn't hurt.

Sam wasn't sure she'd see the ski group again, but a few runs later she found herself turning down a new trail and there they were, the same gold embroidered on blue jackets, the same gorgeous man with the spiderweb skins hugging his thighs. She knew the men in her office complained she didn't take direction well, but that only meant she didn't fawn over their half-baked ideas. If a coach with an ass like that ever wanted to instruct her on anything, she was sure he'd find her plenty teachable.

They were going down a racecourse section by section, practicing the moves they'd been working on before. Blue and red flags flapped in the breeze, the gates spaced out over even intervals. Sam stayed at the top and watched the girls ski. The coach called to them as they went, giving notes about where to shift their weight, offering praise when they got to the bottom. It made Sam think, with both a smile and a pang, about her father, how he used to push her and encourage her at the same time. For a while after he died she thought she'd never be able to put her skis on again.

But here she was, surrounded by bright fields of snow, and she knew the young women on this team were going to remember their coach's words for the rest of their lives.

The last one to tackle the gates was far and away the best. It wasn't only that she was faster. It was more the way she carried herself. She didn't ski like the coach, relaxed even when his muscles were straining. She skied with fierceness, desperate to spring free.

"Forward!" the coach called. "Push down through your toes!"

The girl shifted and everything erupted in front of Sam's eyes. The girl flew in the air, her boots ejected from the skis. Her body was a blur of color as she somersaulted and landed with a thud.

The coach and the rest of the team were well below the fallen girl. Sam sprang into action and skied down. She pulled to a stop and popped out of her skies next to the girl. She had on a helmet, thankfully, but there was blood on her face and a bright smear of it across the snow.

"Are you okay?" Sam asked as she knelt down. The girl's

shoulders racked with sobs and Sam couldn't tell if she was nodding or simply shaking all over.

"Say something," Sam prodded.

"I'm fine," the girl choked.

Sam wasn't convinced, but she waved down to the coach, who was shouting, "Amelia!" in a panic and trying to climb up to reach her.

"She's okay," Sam called, and turned back to the girl. "Is it broken? How much does it hurt?" She helped her sit up and fished in her pocket for a tissue.

Amelia pulled off her gloves and touched around her nose. "I don't think I broke anything. I've done that before. This doesn't feel like that."

"Press the tissue around the bridge to stop the bleeding," Sam instructed.

"You don't have to stay," Amelia said. "Tell Austin it's fine."

"Austin?" Sam asked. She tried not to let her panic register. There could be plenty of people in Gold Mountain named Austin. Maybe even more than one coach by that name.

But she knew it was unlikely.

Fuck.

"My coach," Amelia said. "He'll go crazy if he thinks I'm injured."

"It's too late, he seems to already be losing it. Nothing's broken!" Sam called down the hill. She had to act normally. She couldn't very well introduce herself to him this way, without any of the power of her company name behind her.

At least she was wearing a helmet and ski clothes. If she showed up to a meeting in a suit, heels, and her game face on, she doubted he'd recognize her.

It wasn't like he was paying attention to her anyway. Sam's reassurances had only made Austin redouble his efforts to climb up the mountain on his skis. It wasn't until Sam got an unsteady Amelia back on her feet that he stopped and waited for them to ski down.

They pulled into a hockey stop next to him. "Let me see," he said, and gently lifted away the bloodied wad of tissue, one hand holding Amelia's face, the other pressing around the bridge of her nose to see if she winced. Finally he shook his head. "I'm afraid it's just as I suspected."

Amelia's eyes widened. Austin heaved a dramatic sigh. "It looks like it's going to be death by bloody nose."

Amelia whacked him.

"Your punching muscles work, so you must be okay," he said, then looked over to Sam with a smile. "Thanks for helping. I really appreciate it."

So he was gorgeous, athletic, funny, *and* incredibly kind? Sam wished she were the one submitting to his ministrations—minus the bloody nose and the whole part about having to relive high school while busting her ass on a competitive ski team.

She was going to have to rethink her entire approach to this meeting. She didn't think strong-arming him was going to work. She wasn't even sure she'd be able to do it. He'd distract her just by walking in the door. She'd completely lose her usual edge.

She could use this to her advantage, though. When she saw him later, why not act surprised and introduce herself as the woman who helped him on the mountain? He might realize she wasn't some monster threatening his turf. He might decide there was, in fact, a price she could offer that would make him change his mind.

"It's no problem," Sam said warmly and put a hand on Amelia's shoulder. "Are you sure you're okay?"

Amelia sniffled, not quite nodding, not quite saying no, either.

"You were getting your weight down," Austin said, demonstrating on his own skis. "It felt different because you were in the right position on that last turn. We'll practice holding it so you can get used to how to take that corner with speed."

"Okay. But I'm still gushing blood?" Amelia held up the crimson wad of tissues growing less useful by the minute.

Austin lifted his goggles, squinting down the trail at the girls waiting at the base of the run. Sam had been eager to see what he looked like, but as soon as she saw him she had to dart her eyes away, her cheeks warm in the cold bite of air. Austin didn't just ski beautifully. He *was* beautiful, with large green eyes and a strong jaw accentuated by a short beard that drew attention to his lips. The two stern worry lines wrinkling his brow only added to the picture. If Sam had been in the middle of a turn when she first saw the face that went with that body, she wasn't sure she'd have been able to keep her legs up.

But if he noticed Sam staring, he didn't show it. He was entirely focused on his charge. "You know I can't cut you loose before the bus comes," he said.

"Come *on*." Amelia scowled. "I can take care of myself."

"I know you can. But you're seventeen and a student, and I'm still responsible for you."

"What if I take her inside?" Sam interjected. She was trying to make a good impression, but it was more than that. The kid was bleeding, and Austin's hands were tied.

Amelia and Sam both turned to look at her. "I don't mind," she went on. "The lifts are going to close soon anyway."

Austin was already saying no, but Amelia begged him. "I'll have someone there, so it's not like you let me go early," she argued.

Austin looked at Sam. She could tell he was torn. "Promise me you're not some crazy kidnapper?"

"What if you take my number?" Sam offered, pulling out her phone as though her motives were *totally* selfless. "We'll go down to the lodge and get cleaned up, and by the time you guys are done with practice we'll be ready to go."

Sam thought Austin might not have a phone on him, since everything fit him so well there was no place he could hide yet another bulge. But he pulled off a glove, worn and wrapped with duct tape around the fingers and across the palm, and unzipped the pocket of his vest. Out came a small, beat-up flip phone.

"It's Sam," she said after she took his number and texted him hers.

"Oh, right." Austin grinned over that minor detail he'd forgotten. "I'm Austin."

Sam grinned back. "I know."

His smile seemed to light a flame in her, a warmth that started in her core and blazed out. She had to remind herself she needed his cell number for *work*—not to get in his bed. She'd better not forget to change her voicemail greeting, so he wouldn't wind up with a nasty surprise if he called. Keeping the upper hand meant controlling all information. He'd know her full name when she was good and ready to tell.

Then he reached out to shake her hand, and she felt good and ready for something far different from the meeting she'd come here to schedule with him. It felt foolish that such a simple thing could make her pulse play tricks, but there was no denying it—his touch alone made her heart trip over itself. His skin was warm but in a pleasant way. It reminded her of how he skied, how strong he was.

By now Sam wished she weren't wearing ski pants and a helmet. Or surrounded by a ring of teenage girls ogling them. Or preparing to meet him in a totally different setting, where he wouldn't be nearly as happy to be shaking her hand.

The reminder of why she was here helped bring Sam back

to reality. She dropped his hand.

"Well, that settles that," she said. "We'll be inside. See you in a few. Amelia?"

They skied down and went into the lodge. Amelia headed straight for the bathroom. Sam paused. Should she follow? Leave her alone? But Amelia didn't give her a choice. "If you're my babysitter, then aren't you supposed to be coming?" she called without turning around.

Sam had just wanted a quiet day away from the office before meeting with the elusive Mr. Reede. A Mr. Reede who was supposed to be difficult and recalcitrant but would ultimately prove amenable to reason. Not a Mr. Reede whose green eyes, stubble, and thigh muscles made reason vanish from her mind. How had she gotten into this mess?

Still, she wet paper towels and gave them to Amelia, who wiped the blood crusting around her nostrils and blotted her puffy eyes. "Why are you being so nice?" she asked.

"*Me?*" Sam was used to people calling her plenty of things, but nice wasn't one that usually got a lot of airtime.

Amelia laughed. "You're like Austin, way too nice to people. He's always trying to take care of everyone on the team, and now you're like—you don't even know me but you stopped skiing to help me. Nice, you know?"

Sam shrugged. Was she nice? Really?

Her phone vibrated in her pocket. She'd turned it off silent, and now she pulled it out, thinking it was Austin. But of course there was no such luck. Another text message from Jim. *Why* had she ever gotten into bed with him?

She knew why, and it was two words: "pinot" and "noir." Before she knew it, the whole thing had spiraled out of control. But when she saw his name pop up on her phone, the first thing she thought of wasn't his wide face or his booming voice or his hand on the small of her back, steering her around a room as though she were the prize and not the reason all those CEOs were congregated in the first place.

No, the thing that came to mind was stubble on a strong jaw and green eyes pierced with concern.

"Is that my coach?" Amelia asked, as though Sam had a giant AUSTIN sign flashing over her head. For all Sam knew, she did. Every girl on the team must have had a raging crush on him. They must know exactly what Austin-face looked like.

Sam shook her head to rid herself of thoughts of Austin and his beard scraping her skin. "No."

Amelia raised an eyebrow. "Is it your boyfriend?"

"No," Sam said way too fast. "Definitely not."

"Everyone thinks Austin's crazy hot. I won't tell your boyfriend you looked."

Sam felt all the air rush out of her lungs. "I swear, I don't have a boyfriend."

She didn't know why she said that. It was true, as of six that morning, but it wasn't this kid's business. At all.

"You?" Sam asked, trying to get the focus off her and her now nonexistent love life.

Amelia rolled her eyes. "Like I have time for anything but skiing."

She turned back to the mirror, wiping the last streak of red from her cheek. But before Sam could ask whether Amelia *wanted* time for something besides skiing, the door swung open and a gaggle of girls burst through.

"What *happened* to you?" one girl cried, eyeing her up and down while another poked her head out of the bathroom and shouted, "She's here." In seconds the bathroom was filled with clothes and chatter as the girls changed out of their gear.

"There's no way it's going to be enough to beat Westford," one girl complained as she balled up her long johns.

"You don't know that," came a voice from one of the stalls. "The race isn't for another week."

Another girl checked Amelia on the hip. "You'll be ready,

right?"

"Totally," Amelia said with complete confidence. "We're going to kill it."

Sam moved toward the door, away from the tornado of limbs and hair. Before she left, Amelia caught her eye in the mirror. "Thank you," she mouthed as she brushed her hair.

"You're welcome," Sam said, but Amelia had already turned away, drawn in by a circle of friends ogling a text message one of them had gotten during practice. It made Sam think of the texts waiting for her from Jim, and she stifled a groan. Maybe she could delete them all without reading. Maybe she could set fire to her phone.

She opened the door and walked across the lodge, thinking of her father, her own childhood friends, long hours spent gossiping after school. Once it had felt like time was dragging on forever, but now so many things had ended. It felt like her life would never be the same.

It must have been after four—she could see through the giant windows that the lifts had stopped running. She'd get her stuff, check in to the hotel, and then catch up on the work she'd missed. And when she was sure Austin was home, she'd call and say it was time for them to meet. His home phone, or his cell phone? Well, she had time to decide. She'd run it by Steven and figure out how to proceed.

She was pushing out the double doors back to the snowy outside, trying to remember where she'd left her skis, when she felt a nudge on her shoulder. "Leaving already?"

She almost didn't recognize him without his helmet on. His hair was dirty blond and messy in that perfect "I rolled out of bed looking this good" way Sam could never pull off. His beard was short, brown along his jaw, dusted lighter blond around his lips. His face was serious, hard, but when he smiled his eyes transformed, the edge in him softened but never entirely gone.

The nudge Sam had felt had been his forearm, because both his hands were full. He extended her a steaming paper cup.

"I didn't get to thank you properly," Austin said. "Unless you have to be somewhere?" Those worry lines in his forehead came back.

She should tell him. Tell him now. *Actually, it's funny that we ran into each other like this, since I'd been hoping to meet with you. I didn't properly introduce myself. I'm Samantha Kane.*

But then his face would harden, those bright, hopeful eyes would turn cold, and she didn't want that—not yet.

She took the cup and stepped away from the door. Opposition research, she could call it. And a chance to enjoy her day just a little bit more before she went back to her real life, the one where she was the wolf at whom nobody smiled this way. "Nope, nowhere to be," she said. "And I'd love to be thanked properly."

Chapter Three

He was nowhere near as smooth as he'd imagined. Instead of him sitting there, relaxed, offering Sam a seat, basking in her smile as she saw the cocoa, he'd almost missed her and had to chase her down. Like he was desperate. Like he didn't get that she had places to be. Just because she'd been nice enough to bring Amelia in didn't mean she'd do anything but walk out the door.

But she wasn't busy. And she even smiled at him. They sat across from each other next to the enormous windows that opened to the white of the trails. The late-afternoon sun streamed through, turning her brown hair gold. Sam had taken off her perfectly fitted ski jacket to reveal a trim black wool sweater with enough hint of a white layer that all he wanted was to pull it off and see what else she had on underneath.

Damn, he moved fast in his mind.

Relationships had an unfortunate way of getting personal, and no one needed to know the memories of his injury that still woke him in the night. But he could look. And enjoy.

Which he'd been doing ever since he first caught sight of

the woman skiing down to Amelia and realized she'd clearly been on a mountain before. What he noticed second, when she got closer and lifted her goggles, was that she'd look good off skis as well. She'd look good in just about anything.

Or, for that matter, nothing at all.

She was tall, with dark eyes and finely arched brows. Austin had felt himself grow hot under her gaze, his panic at Amelia's fall giving way to a different kind of adrenaline surge. When she'd taken his hand, the electric shock of her touch hit him so hard he could barely concentrate for the girls' last two runs.

Austin wasn't used to losing his focus. It was just him, the snow, the skis. But he wasn't out on the mountain now, climbing to take off on a backcountry run. He wasn't even worrying about that obnoxious call from Steven Park. He was doing what he never did, which was sit around the lodge and drink overpriced, too-sweet hot chocolate. Why, he wasn't sure.

"So do you always go around saving people on the slopes?" he asked, blowing on the steaming cocoa.

"Only when I get lucky." The corners of her lips rose—almost a smile, but not quite. He wondered what he'd have to do to earn a real one. "What about you? Is coaching always so dramatic?"

Austin shook his head. He wished he could have met her when he hadn't been wearing a helmet for hours. He'd tried to smooth down his hair in the bathroom, but the situation was beyond help. She, though, had the perfect tousled look, long strands swept to the side, just loose enough to make him think how appealing she'd be if she really came undone.

He took a sip of cocoa, trying to keep composed. "I keep everyone upright as best I can. But Amelia…" He sighed. "I don't know. Her times are good, but she's been off recently. I don't know how to get her back on track."

"She'll be okay," Sam said. "She's a great skier. They all are."

"State semifinals six years and counting."

"Wow!" Sam's eyebrows shot up.

He laughed. "Actually that's not so good—we used to win sometimes."

"But it sounded from the team like you guys are doing well this year."

"I know, they've got a real shot at advancing to the next round."

"And Amelia?" Sam asked.

"I've never trained anyone like her." It wasn't one of those platitudes teachers liked to say. Amelia really was the best student he'd ever had. "There's no question she'll be in the finals for the individual slots, even if the whole team doesn't come through. The bigger deal is that she's being recruited for a competition in Utah that will go toward determining spots on the national team. I have a feeling she can make it as far as she wants." He paused. "She just has to want to, of course."

Sam frowned and put down the cup. "Too much pressure?"

"I didn't use to think so. Now?" He played with the plastic lid. The cocoa was too sweet, but he always forgot how much he liked it anyway. "I wish I knew."

Sam gave him a sympathetic look. "She'll figure it out."

He smiled, embarrassed by how long he'd gone on about the team. "Sorry, too much yammering on my part. The girls are always telling me to talk about something else. Where are you in from? Here for the day?"

"I live in Seattle," Sam said, which was what he'd guessed.

"Do you come here a lot?"

"To Gold?" She shook her head. "Not recently. I used to come with my father, but I—" Her voice caught, and she looked away. "I haven't been up in a few years."

"You picked a great day to do it—actual sun in the winter

is a miracle. Although I hear it's supposed to start coming down tonight."

"Snow?" Sam turned back to him in surprise. "But it's not even cloudy."

"That's the mountains for you. You can't predict a thing around here."

As if on cue, the bathroom doors shot open, and the team spilled out. They were chattering about whatever had happened at school when a voice that could only be Kelsey's carried over the group. "Shut. Up."

They all stopped, staring at Austin and Sam, and then erupted in a volley of giggles.

"You've never seen anyone drink cocoa before?" he demanded.

But that only made them laugh harder and they scrambled out of the lodge, singing, "'Byeeeeee, Austin! 'Bye, Sam!" as they pushed open the door.

How was it possible to be a grown-ass man and still mortified by high school girls?

"I really should get going," Sam said as she followed the parade of girls with her eyes.

Inside, Austin cursed. But he said, "Of course. I didn't mean to keep you."

"You didn't keep me. I just—work doesn't quite know I'm taking the day off, so I should check in." Sam waved a hand dismissively as though that covered it. No rings, he noticed. Wedding or otherwise. Nails manicured with some sort of clear, shiny polish but no other marks.

"Of course," Austin said again, then wished he could expand his vocabulary beyond those two words. And make himself stop staring at her. "Well...thanks again for your help. I appreciated it."

Sam nodded. She put on her jacket and tucked her face mask and goggles into her helmet to carry. For one crazy second, Austin opened his mouth to ask where she was staying, if he could call her, what she was doing tonight.

But she was the one saying good-bye. Clearly she wanted to go. She probably had someone in Seattle anyway. She carried herself with an understated confidence, not egotistical but certainly not shying away. Surely there was some successful city guy who knew how to sweep her off her feet.

"So, have a great rest of the day," Austin said.

"Thanks, good luck with the race. And thanks for the cocoa, too."

"Any time."

He couldn't tell if she was lingering or simply zipping up her coat, but after another smile she walked out the door and was gone.

Austin took one last sip of lukewarm cocoa and trashed the rest. He tried to tell himself it was for the best. Any time he wound up interested in someone, he inevitably found a way to push her away. That was his pattern, his thing. Ever since his father brought down that hammer and shattered both Austin's knee and his world, it was too hard to let anyone in. If he really liked Sam, he'd let her walk away.

Besides, he had too many other things to worry about. Like how many voicemails he was going to have from Steven Park when he got home. And what he was going to say when he finally met Samantha Kane. She had to accept that he wasn't selling a single tree from his land.

If she didn't like it, that was her problem. Not his.

Chapter Four

Austin came home to a hungry dog and a sore knee—and, surprisingly, not a single message. He tried to focus on dinner, the next day's practice, what he was going to do to get Amelia's spark back. But getting Sam out of his mind was easier said than done. He kept returning to the sweep of her hair and the way her brown eyes crinkled when she smiled, like it wasn't just a gesture her face did but something she actually meant.

He wasn't sure if she was staying overnight, but as he stood under the shower, he kicked himself for not finding out. He didn't have to go planning their breakup in his head when they hadn't even gotten together. *When are you going back to Seattle? Are you seeing anyone? Would you like to have dinner tonight?* A million questions, none of them hard. He should have just picked one and asked.

He shut the water off. He knew better than anyone that there was no use rehashing the past. But he hadn't gotten in any more skiing after practice and he was restless—too wired with thoughts of Sam's lithe body to settle down for the night. He started in on a round of stretches his friend Claire, a massage therapist, had shown him to help with his knee. He blamed her for all this *thinking*. She was the first one to point out that his string of failed romances had one common denominator—him. But was that going to keep him from ever trying anything when a beautiful woman came his way?

Austin opened the fridge, closed it, and grabbed the keys to his truck. He had to get out of the house. Otherwise he might find himself calling Steven Park just to give himself something to do.

Chloe's ears perked up from her bed. "Oh, live a little," he admonished the dog. "It's Tuesday! Why can't we have any fun?"

Chloe seemed to think for a minute, then nudged her nose back down to rest.

"Fine," Austin said. "You stay home and keep the Kanes away. But don't wait up, okay?"

Chloe's ear flicked. She was already asleep.

Tuesdays meant two-for-one beers at the Dipper, the local watering hole everyone called Mack Daddy's after the bartender, Mackenzie Ellinsworth. The name enraged the chef, Connor Branding, who claimed he was the reason anyone showed up at the Dipper at all. But even though Connor was Austin's best friend, Mack had worked there longer, and Austin couldn't help thinking of the joint as hers.

The parking lot was mostly empty, but that was to be expected on a weeknight, just a few trucks built for snow and then, inexplicably, a silver Audi that was going to be unhappy if it stuck around once the storm started up. Austin had been right—the day's blue sky had turned to clouds as the sun set. Now the darkness was deepening, and he could feel the damp promise of snow in the air. If it kept up through the night, tomorrow's tracks were going to be good.

He lingered in the parking lot, watching the first flakes begin to settle, before kicking the slush and salt off his boots and stepping inside. As usual Mack was behind the bar. She waved as he walked in.

"Long time no see!" she called, and Austin laughed. He'd been there last night, playing poker with Connor after closing.

"What'll it be?" she asked, grabbing a glass.

"You still have the Black Raven?"

Austin stood at the bar, and Mack poured the ale. He was taking his first sip when he felt a nudge on his arm.

He nearly spit his drink all over the bar. What was *she* doing here?

Sam had showered and changed from the afternoon, her hair no longer tousled by the helmet but smoothed in a sideways part and pulled back. She was wearing jeans and a sweater, so he could see what her ski pants had only hinted at. "Cute" didn't seem like the right word—she had a way of carrying herself that was too self-assured for that. Beautiful felt like a cliché. What actually ran through his mind was *fucking hot*, but that made him sound like a caveman, so he tried to tame it down.

Still, that was all he could think of. Fucking hot.

"Fancy meeting you here," she said with a wink.

"I had no idea you were sticking around. Did you get some work done?"

"A little. I was supposed to have some meetings, but I was able to push everything back."

"You two know each other?" Mack asked, refilling Sam's glass.

"Um—"

Austin started to speak as Sam said, "We met this afternoon."

Austin flashed Mack a look that he hoped said *keep your*

big mouth shut. "Where are you staying?" he asked Sam.

"Up at the Cascade," she said.

Austin and Mack exchanged glances. The Cascade was the one fancy hotel on the mountain, so expensive only the wealthiest Seattleites stayed there. Usually they never left to venture into the cluster of businesses and shops that made up the actual town. They definitely never came into Mack's.

"I know," Sam said, as though she could read their look. "The place is ridiculous. Someone needs to break it to them that the seventies ended a few years back. That wallpaper is a crime."

"They've got a nice bar, though," Mack said, and Austin could hear the envy in her voice. Mack wanted a real bar. Not the three rotating kegs and tub of well drinks at the Dipper, but a place where she could make infused syrups and herbal concoctions and have full control over which eighteen kinds of local gin to buy.

"I popped my head in and it looked decent," Sam said, "but even the guy at the front desk told me to come here instead."

Mack's eyebrows rocketed up. She never failed to show what she was thinking. "I'm shocked they acknowledged anything outside the hotel."

"Me, too," Sam said. "But I said I wanted to see what the area was like, and this was where they sent me. Looks like it must be where everybody hangs out, if I ran into this one again." She raised her glass toward Austin.

"You had a one in three chance of getting it right," Mack said. "The mountain, the gym in his freaky basement, or here."

"Sounds like a wild kind of guy."

Mack laughed. "You have no idea."

"Hey," Austin interjected. "I'm standing right here."

"Maybe you should grab a seat, then." Mack gestured toward the tables.

"And leave you alone at the bar?" Austin teased.

"I'm not alone, I have Connor back there being an asshole."

"Who's Connor?" Sam asked.

"My best friend," Austin said, at the same time Mack grumbled, "The worst ever." They stared at each other for a beat and burst out laughing.

A voice called out from the back, "Not to mention maker of the best beet burger you've never had!"

Sam stared at them both. "He heard what you said?"

"Trust me," Mack said, wiping her eyes. "He's heard worse."

Connor popped out of the door between the bar and the kitchen. "Don't listen to a word she says," he said, nodding toward Mack. "She doesn't even know how good a beet burger can be."

"I hate beets!" Mack roared so loudly the other patrons dotting the restaurant turned and stared. She glared at Connor. "Get back in your kitchen hole."

"And get me a flesh burger," Austin called before his friend could disappear again. He turned to Sam. "They have an actual menu—I swear you don't have to shout your order."

Sam slapped her hand on the bar. "I want the beet burger."

Connor grinned. "It's not an official item, but you're going to be a very happy guinea pig."

"Go, get out of here," Mack said to Sam as though it pained her. "Enjoy your last minutes before your dirt meal."

Sam grabbed her beer and walked away, then stopped and turned. "Coming?"

Austin hadn't realized what she'd meant. He always sat at the bar, chatting with Mack, calling to Connor when he was busy in the kitchen.

But who was he to turn down Sam's invitation? She was beautiful, sharp, fun, and hadn't seemed fazed by his friends.

Who else could he say that about? He followed her to where she'd been sitting before he walked in. She had a laptop on the table and a stack of papers, but she quickly swept everything away.

"You sure I'm not interrupting?"

"I don't want to be doing this anyway." She gestured for him to sit.

"What are you working on?" he asked, but she had her phone out and was sending a message.

"Just some sales stuff," she said, not looking up from her phone. "Totally boring." She put the phone down. "Sorry. So it seems like you come here a lot?"

They talked about the bar, the mountain, the area, Austin's friends. "You work in sales?" he asked when he felt he'd gone on long enough.

"Real estate, actually. But it's nothing that can't wait."

Austin could tell she didn't want to talk about it. But could he blame her? A chance to get out of the office and have an excuse not to work through dinner, and here he was trying to ask her more about it. He switched tracks.

"So how often do you usually get to hit the snow?"

She shook her head sheepishly, smoothing a lock of hair that had dropped from where it was pulled back. "Not often enough. I used to go a few times a year, which probably doesn't sound like much to you but felt like a lot to me."

"What changed?"

"Oh." Her eyes fluttered up from her beer to him. He could see her searching his face. "I used to go with my father."

"Really?" Austin tried to picture a father who skied—who did things with his kid at all. He knew that kind of thing existed. Of course it did. But you didn't meet too many people who got that wistful pang in their eye when they talked about their parents. He felt a sudden throb in his knee and massaged it under the table, pressing his thumb to the tender spot that acted up whenever the weather changed. But he knew not to show the pain on his face.

"He was the only one I ever skied with, actually. I have it so permanently associated with him in my mind that it was hard when I—that I didn't do a lot of—" She looked away.

"I'm sorry," Austin said. "It sounds like a tremendous loss."

Sam nodded. She looked saddened by what he'd just said, but also—he hoped—relieved not to have to say the words.

"How long ago?" he asked softy.

"Three years today, but sometimes it still feels like yesterday."

He raised his glass. "I'm glad you came."

She clinked his glass with hers and took a sip. "I'm glad I came, too." She smiled. "Are your parents skiers? I bet you were on skis since before you could walk."

"Actually, it was an uncle who got me started. He used to swing by to get me out of the house. And since we lived in Colorado, I guess he decided to stick me on skis."

"And then you raced? Professionally? I mean, before you started to coach."

Maybe it was the beer, or the intensity in her eyes, or the fact that she'd been open about her father and her grief, that led him to tell her what he so rarely talked about. It had taken him ages to work up to admitting it to Connor when they first met. If Mack knew, it was only because someone else had told her. But he could be honest with Sam without telling her the whole story.

"I was expected to medal at the Salt Lake City Olympics," he admitted.

Sam's jaw literally dropped.

"And then what?"

He shrugged. "I didn't medal."

"Shit happens."

He laughed. "Yeah, I guess so."

"Did you finish the runs?"

"I didn't even start. Injured two weeks before."

"You're kidding."

Austin raised his glass. "To bad timing. And even worse knees."

"Wow," Sam said. And then again, "Wow."

He liked her reaction. No pity, no comfort. Just the facts.

"I wasn't sure I'd ever ski again," he went on. "But moving here, it's the perfect place for me. It's away from the major training circuits in the Rockies, but I still get talented kids from Gold Mountain. After everything that happened I wanted to be out of the spotlight, you know?"

"Of course. You do what you love." She smiled. "My dad was so driven, so good at everything he did, it was nice he had a hobby. Something he did because he enjoyed it, not because he had to or because he expected anything in return. I'm not sure I can imagine skiing every day, though."

"It becomes part of your schedule. Like someone else might go for a run or, I don't know, knit a sweater."

Sam laughed at the analogy. "We used to go during my school vacations. Sometimes I resented it because I wanted to be with my friends, but as an adult it felt special, getting to spend all that time with my dad."

No matter how hard Austin tried to picture what she was telling him, he couldn't. Parents who went on vacation? Together? All the yelling in his house was bad enough—he couldn't imagine it in a hotel room.

He drained his beer. Better to keep the focus on her. "Did you come here a lot?"

"Some, if he wanted to pop up for a weekend or even a day trip if the weather was good. But he loved the big places—Taos, Vail, Park City."

Austin had already guessed her family had money to

burn. "This must have seemed like such a podunk place to him," he said with a laugh, trying to hide his discomfort.

He was surprised when Sam shook her head. "He loved the mountain, the proximity to Seattle, how beautiful it is up here. He always talked about the potential in this area."

Austin could feel his face darkening. "That's what the developers keep talking about. Those fucking Kanes are going to gut this place, all in the name of 'potential.'"

He saw Sam stiffen. On second thought, maybe he shouldn't have cursed.

"I'm sorry," he said. "I'm a little bitter."

"Why?" she asked with a frown.

"Long story short, I own some land that I got for cheap when I moved here. Nothing huge," he added, lest she get the wrong idea. "But Kane Enterprises wants to buy a chunk of it to turn into condos. Let's just say 'over my dead body' isn't an exaggeration."

"They must be offering a good buyout, though," Sam countered. "I mean, I'm sure the people at the company aren't unreasonable. There's nothing that could change your mind?"

She cocked her head at him expectantly, but Austin shook his head. "I'm not for sale."

Sam was about to respond when her phone buzzed. She pulled it off the table and angled it down as she scrolled through the message. Austin was reminded of how the girls sat with their phones in their laps when they watched videos of their races, as though no one would notice when they weren't paying attention. He thought about his indecision in the lodge, how if it wasn't for her showing up tonight he would have let her get away. He leaned across the table.

"Is that your boyfriend?" he asked.

"What?" Sam looked up.

Austin nodded toward the phone. "Just wondering who the lucky guy is who's got your attention tonight."

She made a face. "You should know I'm in a long-term relationship with my job. But don't worry. We're not monogamous."

She made a show of darkening the screen and sliding it into her bag behind her. "Out of sight, out of mind."

So no boyfriend, and intentions that couldn't be clearer. The look she gave him, a half smile, her head tilted so he could see the soft side of her neck, the arc of her jaw, her hair spilling over her shoulder—Austin felt himself growing hard right there under the table. He leaned closer. "I don't want to make anyone jealous."

"Are we really having the monogamy talk before you've even—"

Fucked me, he thought she was going to say. He hoped she was going to say. His dick strained up, expecting her to say it.

But there was a clatter from the kitchen as the door opened and Mack restarted her usual diatribe against Connor. Sam pressed her lips together, not finishing the thought. But under the table he felt the pressure of her leg slide against his, making sure he knew what she'd meant.

And he definitely did. Everything—*everything*—in him stiffened at her touch. He shifted in the seat as Connor came over with their plates.

"Two burgers at your service," he said. "One extra delicious"—he pointed to Sam's—"and one my usual mediocrity."

"And yet your mediocrity is still the best thing going in this town," Austin commented. For the first time, he hoped Connor wouldn't join him, because he couldn't ignore the bulge in his pants or the curve of the lips of the woman before him. But Connor seemed to get the hint.

"Bon appétit." He flashed Austin a quick grin before ducking away.

"Please come back even if it's bad," Mack called to Sam from the bar. Connor flipped her off before retreating into the kitchen.

Austin looked at Sam as she surveyed her plate. "You didn't have to do that just to be nice," he said.

"You know, you're the second person today who's called me that," Sam said. "And the second to ask if I have a boyfriend."

Austin stopped spreading mustard midsmear. "Do I have competition?"

She laughed. "It was just Amelia being nosy."

Austin narrowed his eyes. "And what did you tell her?"

"To quit pointing out how hot you are. I have eyes myself."

She grinned and dived into her burger before Austin could manage a response. When she finished chewing, her eyes were wide.

"That," she said, pointing to her plate, "is dynamite. Taste this."

"You're not trying to poison me, are you?"

Sam brushed his leg again under the table. "One thing you should know about me," she said in a low voice. "I don't fuck around."

She held his eyes for so long it was almost disconcerting. He'd never want to cross this woman. He pictured her making deals, some nebulous, confusing thing she did for a living with that phone practically glued to her hands. She was obviously someone who got what she wanted, whatever it was.

He hoped for tonight that would be him.

He reached for her burger and took a bite. Not exactly a sexy meal, but he couldn't help feeling a thrill about placing his mouth where hers had just been.

"Holy shit," he said when he finished chewing.

"I know, right?"

"But that's good." Austin stated the obvious. "That's

really good."

Connor poked his head out of the kitchen. "Are my ears burning?"

"They will be if you keep coming out here instead of paying attention to what you're cooking," Mack said, and then added, "You guys, stop making things up."

"I'm not kidding. This is amazing," Austin said before Connor went back to the kitchen. He suddenly felt terrible for all the times he'd joined with Mack in teasing his friend.

As they finished their meals, Sam chided Austin and Mack for not seeing what Connor had been offering them.

"I guess you get used to things," Austin said. "You see the same people every day and you think you know what they're about, what they do. And then it turns out you have no idea."

"It's not that you didn't know," Sam said. "It's not like he's somebody different. Now you happen to know more about him."

"If you pay attention," Austin said. He looked at Sam, at the way her eyes widened and narrowed as she spoke, her expression always shifting. Her voice was strong and firm, calling him out but in a way that made him feel like she cared, even though it had been only hours, really, that they'd known each other. *I'm paying attention*, he thought to himself. *I want to know more about you.*

"They're scared," Austin said quietly, not wanting Mack to hear.

Sam's brows pressed together. "Of what? Success?"

Austin shook his head. "I'm not the only one personally affected by the Kane takeover. My friends are lucky not to be in the direct path of the development, but still. Everything they know is about to be taken away."

Sam sat up so straight he could see what she probably looked like in a suit, the blade of a knife pressed flush against her spine. "You don't know that," she said.

"The owners of Gold Mountain and every landowner for miles around are selling everything—except for me, that is. You don't think that's going to bring changes?"

"But why do you assume those changes will be bad?"

"You obviously haven't seen the plans. Sure, everybody wants more skiable acreage. But massive expansion means tons of trees cut down, more snowmaking, and the Kanes have given no indication they know or even care about how to make any of that sustainable. Four new luxury hotels, hundreds of condos—half of them in my backyard—and then there are the restaurants and stores you need to support the influx of people who'll come up a few days a year, dump their dollars, and leave everyone starving the rest of the time."

"Jobs?" Sam countered. "Opportunities? Convenience? Are you saying you couldn't use a larger supermarket, or a medical center that doesn't require driving to Bellingham?"

He couldn't believe she was parroting the developers' arguments. "I'm not stuck here, if that's what you're getting at. I live in the woods because I like it. I may not be able to stop the development outright, but that doesn't mean I have to cave."

He thought she was going to disagree, come back with some line that would make him even more incensed. But instead she cocked her head and looked at him like she was reading something printed in the back of his mind that even he couldn't see.

"What?" he asked warily.

But all she said was, "Here, have the last bite of my burger. You've been skiing all day and I'm stuffed."

Austin reached for the burger, but he wished he were reaching across the table for her instead. She'd pulled her leg away, and he felt the emptiness. All he wanted was to get it back.

Chapter Five

Wonderful, he was wonderful.

And so incredibly *not* an option.

She hadn't meant to flirt so hard with him. But once he started asking about work, she had to get him off the subject. So she'd traced her leg along the inside of his calf, pushing aside the voice telling her the responsible thing was to get up, thank him for the evening, and go. Since the responsible thing would have been to make their first and *only* meeting professional, clearly responsible was off the table for tonight.

The problem was that in distracting him, she'd also distracted herself. For one sweet second she'd forgotten why she was there, and what she needed from him.

Until he had to bring up her company again.

Prior to meeting him, she'd assumed Mr. Reede's obstinacy had to do with money, pride, stubbornness—something she could reason with or overcome. But it was all about the principle, and keeping his life unchanged. Simply upping her offer wasn't going to make Austin change his mind. And once he found out she'd been essentially lying to him, he'd only be more set against her, her family, and her father's dream.

It was time to cool it with the flirting, go back to her hotel, and wake up tomorrow ready to work. At least she could tell Steven she'd made contact. That ought to buy her a little more time with the board.

She gave an exaggerated yawn. "Thanks for the company, but I'm beat. I should go."

"Already?" Austin looked at her with that adorable line of concern settling between his eyes. *He's not on the menu*, Sam warned herself before the scruff on his jaw could make her give in.

"I should get back before the snow sticks on the roads." She signaled to a waitress for the bill and grabbed it before Austin could. She was pulling out her credit card when she realized how stupid that was. Did she want to hand him a business card while she was at it? She stuffed in way too much cash, waving the waitress away when she asked if Sam needed change.

"It's all taken care of," Sam said to Austin when he reached for his wallet, too.

Austin looked at her like she'd just confessed to being overrun with toe fungus. "You can't do that."

"Of course I can. Thanks, Mack," she called. "Tell Connor that beet burger was A-plus. You should try it sometime."

Mack snorted that Connor would probably poison her, and Austin said yeah, except they needed to keep her around to change the beer taps. Sam found herself laughing along with their teasing. She thought about her own nights out with colleagues and the few friends she rarely got to see. If she were back in Seattle she'd still be at work, ordering takeout, too busy going over the numbers again to stop and actually eat.

Outside the snow was coming down hard, coating the parking lot in a layer of white. The weather in Seattle was dependably gray. All they'd gotten this winter was rain and more rain and that dreaded wintry mix. She stood in the middle of the parking lot and tilted her face to the sky.

Snow clung to her lashes and melted down her cheeks. She could see it coming toward her, illuminated by the outdoor lights from the bar, but higher up where the lights didn't reach everything was darkness. The flakes seemed to emerge straight from a dizzying abyss. She felt Austin come up behind her, the solid weight of him dangerously close. She knew how unfair she was being to him, and how much of her job she was putting at risk.

But she couldn't make herself pull away.

"It's beautiful," she said quietly.

"I know."

He pulled out a strand of hair that had gotten tucked in her scarf.

"Where's your hat?" he asked. But it was more like a whisper, his lips brushing close to her ear.

"I forgot it," she said hoarsely. Her mouth was dry.

He ran a hand over her hair, smoothing out the snow. "Do you want mine?"

Sam turned to face him. Her whole life, her whole career, was spent calculating risk versus reward. How much risk could the company assume when they bought new land? How much would they be rewarded for the chance they took?

She knew not every risk wound up being worth it. But zero risk meant zero gain. Wasn't that the whole philosophy that had gotten her father's company where it was? Knowing when to take the plunge. Damn it, Austin was gorgeous, even with a gray wool hat pulled over his ears. And he was funny, thoughtful, kind—

She wrapped her gloved hands around his scarf and pressed her lips to his.

There was a pause in which he seemed surprised—was

she wrong? Surely he wanted this, too. And then his arms were around her and he was kissing her back. The voice in her head stating firmly that this was a very bad idea tasted sweetness and warmth, and for a moment there was only silence. The world, her mind, even the wind itself had gone still.

Then a burst of noise came from behind them. A couple walked out of the bar and headed to their car. It was the reminder Sam needed. Nothing about their situation had changed. She couldn't get caught up in the romance of the falling snow.

"I should go," she said, pulling away.

"I'll walk you to your car."

Sam laughed. The parking lot wasn't exactly big enough to get lost in. She pulled out her keys and unlocked the Audi. It beeped, and the lights flashed.

"Oh, no." Austin groaned.

"You can't walk me that far?"

"Did you forget it's snowing?" He held up his palms, catching the flakes.

"So?"

"So you can't drive that thing in the snow."

Sam glared at him. "I drive *that thing* everywhere."

"Not on dark, windy mountain roads on nights like this. Get in the truck."

"Which one?" she asked, looking around the lot. "They're all trucks."

"Exactly. Because people around here know how to drive in winter."

"Ugh, what is it about men and cars?"

"I'm sorry, I'm just not that good at forgiving myself when I find out people I've been enjoying a perfectly lovely evening with wind up skidding off the road. Must be a man thing."

"Lovely evening?" She raised an eyebrow.

"I take it back, I'm having a terrible time. Get in anyway

and I'll take you to your hotel."

"I have to work tonight," Sam said pointedly, not making a move toward his truck.

He smiled. "I'm not inviting myself in."

"Are you sure?"

Austin raised his palm. "Scout's honor."

Sam couldn't help herself. "Well, that's disappointing."

Austin dropped his hand immediately. "Good thing I was never a Boy Scout, so my promises don't mean a thing."

Sam tugged on his scarf. It was *so* tempting.

But she had to back away.

"I told you I'm not monogamous with my job," she said. "But it's still my primary relationship, and it's expecting me tonight. Let's go before these papers get wet. I don't think my bag is waterproof."

Austin unlocked his truck and brushed snow off the windshields.

Don't invite him in. Don't invite him in.

Sam tried to strengthen her resolve as he drove.

But Austin didn't give her a chance to turn down any implied invitation.

"I can drive you back to your car when the streets are plowed," he said as he pulled into the circle in front of the Cascade and waved off the valet attendant coming to take the car.

Sam unbuckled her seat belt. "I appreciate it. You're right, that wouldn't have gone so well in my car. You're sure you don't mind picking me up tomorrow?"

"Of course not. You have my cell, right?" Austin patted down his pockets. "I think it's at home now—I'm bad at remembering to keep it with me. But for you, I'll carry the little monitor all day."

It was ridiculous, this mountain man who lived in the woods and went out without a cell phone. But it was attractive, too, the way he gave everything his full attention. Not once had he been distracted from her while they ate. His mind certainly hadn't been anywhere else when they'd kissed.

Sam almost leaned over to do it again, her resolve draining away.

But she wasn't the wolf for no reason. Before she could make an even bigger mistake, she pulled away, grabbed her bag, and slammed the door. She had no doubt he would have followed her in a heartbeat if she'd asked him to. But she couldn't. It wasn't fair, it wasn't right, and there was no way it would end well.

Chapter Six

"Good evening, Ms. Kane." Philip, the manager who'd checked Sam in that afternoon, doffed his hat to her from behind the front desk. Instinctively, Sam jerked around to look behind her, but Austin was already driving away.

Forget taking him to her room, where she was afraid she might have left his file strewn across her bed. Just setting foot near the hotel was risky. She breathed a sigh of relief that she hadn't invited him in.

Her suite was comfortable, if small. Her company's plans for renovating the Cascade involved gutting the top floor to create larger rooms, in addition to the new hotels they were going to build. It was exciting, but Austin's face when he mentioned the Kanes kept flashing before her eyes. Why didn't he see that her project was going to make this area so much better?

But she knew the answer to that. Austin didn't want better. He wanted what he had.

And, it seemed, he wanted her.

Which he wouldn't, as soon as he found out who she was.

She could flirt, she could kiss him in the snow, but Sam hadn't gotten to where she was by being a romantic. She was nothing if not realistic, and she knew it was only a matter of time.

Still, that kiss…

She rolled onto her back. Her fingers moved slowly down her body, over her breasts, traveling south to the heat that came just from thinking his name. God, the memory of his thighs in those racing skins, the scratch of his beard against her cheek—the thought of it grazing between her legs instead… She was going to come in seconds, replaying the electricity that had jolted through her as she brushed her leg against his under the table like some teenager thrilled by the most innocent touch.

But not so innocent—not with how wet she was.

She was sliding her finger right to the place that would make her let go when her phone buzzed. She imagined Austin's voice, husky, just breathless enough to make her want to work him up to a pant. He was going to tell her he'd had a wonderful time that night. He was going to say he never should have driven away.

She was going to tell him, right then, what she was doing while thinking of him.

But the reminder of the hotel manager wishing her a good night stopped her fantasy cold. And then she reached for the phone and saw the number. Not five minutes of a good time and work was calling, like those boys in the office could see when she was getting out of line.

"Kane here," she said with a cough, trying to sound like she'd been hard at work as opposed to mere seconds from an orgasm brought about by dexterous fingers and dirty thoughts.

"Samantha, you okay there? It's Steven checking in."

Sam swung her legs around so she was sitting on the edge of the bed, as though her assistant could hear she was getting too relaxed. "Sure," she said. "Great. Are you still at the office?"

"Everyone is. As I'm sure you can guess, the board is buzzing about your trip."

"What are they saying? How do they even know?"

Sam knew she could count on Steven to be honest, and he was. "Jim started the rumors, and it took off from there. Half of them think it's unprofessional. The other half are reserving judgment until they see if it works."

"In other words, the half that want to keep their jobs if I'm successful, and the favor of the board if I'm not."

"Something like that. What should I report back?"

"I've made contact with Mr. Reede," she said, eyeing herself in the mirror across from the bed. Her hair was undone, her cheeks flushed, her nipples peaked. That was one way of putting it.

"So he'll sign?" Steven asked.

Sam paused. "We didn't broach that yet."

"I'll tell them you're working on it."

"Be clear that we're in touch and moving forward. I have his cell phone, we've met once already, and we have plans to sit down again tomorrow. That ought to buy me some time."

She gave Steven the number for their records but told him she'd be the one to call. Previously the plan had been to show Mr. Reede the full weight of the company Sam carried. Now, she told Steven, she thought the personal approach would be better. "Show him we're regular, well-meaning people just like him."

She wasn't sure he'd buy it. She wasn't sure *she* bought it. But Steven simply verified that she wouldn't be in the office tomorrow and moved on.

"I think the board needs to hear directly from you that everything's proceeding as planned," he said.

"Once Aus—Mr. Reede—signs, I'll go straight to the Hendersons to finalize the last of the sale in person. One more day, maybe two, max."

"Good," he said, "because the Hendersons won't sign away their portion until everything else is set, and we can't get the ski resort without them. I'll let the board know that's coming by the end of the week."

Sam's stomach tightened to hear Steven's timeline. That meant barely any time to see Austin again as someone other than his opponent. But she said, "Thank you, Steven, I don't know what I'd do without you."

"Are you sure you aren't going stir-crazy? We all know there's nothing to do up there."

That had been one of the common refrains in the office, that they were finally going to breathe some life into such a tired part of the state.

Sam forced a laugh. "I think I can handle a day."

She hung up, told her nipples to calm down, and looked over the blueprint again. There was the Cascade, and the lines marking the proposed expansion. There were the condos meant for Austin's land.

The condos that would go where her father had planned, she corrected herself. She'd told Steven her course of action for tomorrow. Now she had to follow through.

It had been fun to be out of the office, but her real life took place far away from here. Not even the taste of Austin's lips was reason to stay.

• • •

Austin racked his brain, reviewing every step of the night. The kiss was good, right? And she was the one who'd initiated it. She would have asked him to her room if she'd wanted to. Yet she very clearly had not.

What he wanted to know was who stayed at the Cascade, anyway. Corporate types, which it looked like she was. No wonder she wasn't outraged at what the Kanes were doing to him. She actually thought the development might be okay. She clearly wasn't the right one for him.

But he wasn't talking about the right one. He was talking about the right one for *tonight*. For a few hours to find out what was beneath that sultry smile as he tasted the snow off her skin.

He couldn't believe she'd been able to say good night to him without a second thought. Surely she hadn't gone straight to bed without thinking maybe she'd made a mistake in letting him go. Not after the way she'd drawn her foot up his leg and fixed her eyes on him at dinner.

There had to be a chance she'd changed her mind.

He checked the kitchen, his bedroom, trying to remember where he'd put his phone. As he'd told Sam, he didn't use it very often. He tried to bring it when he coached, but even then it was haphazard. When he'd left Colorado after finishing rehab, he'd needed distance from his old life. His knee had shattered in a way that called to mind clay pots, broken china, glasses so smashed they were nothing but shards. It was too hard to hear his mother's voice, crying and guilty, begging him to come home. It got to be so that he couldn't stand to hear his cell phone ring and only called her when he felt prepared.

Because that was the one thing he'd never do. He would ski again, despite the doctors' prognosis. But he'd never go home.

He used to call his uncle sometimes, but he'd wanted to talk about the injury, and Austin was trying to heal, not relive the pain. He got so busy with school in Washington and his new life away from the pro-skier circuit that he stopped calling back. It wasn't until he found out his uncle had passed away from a heart attack that Austin understood how much his stubbornness had cost.

He didn't want to be like that anymore, disconnected,

alone, absent when somebody called. He went tearing through his house as Chloe stared at him, head cocked, thoroughly confused. He lived down from the peak, tucked away from the main road that ran in and out of town. It was a small house, but not when he was looking for an even smaller cell phone. It wasn't until he found it under a cushion in the living room that it occurred to him he'd have heard the thing ringing if Sam had called to tell him to come over tonight.

He looked at the blank screen and tossed it on the couch. He shouldn't have let himself get carried away.

He stood in front of the sliding doors in the back of the house and watched the snow fall over the yard. There was just enough of a clearing for Chloe to run in before the woods began, the same woods that rose up the sides of Gold Mountain and spread across the peaks. The same woods Kane Enterprises wanted to take from him and tear down.

"We'll figure it out," he said to Chloe when she came up next to him, looking through the glass as the snow filled in their tracks from earlier that day. He wasn't sure if he was talking about Sam or the Kanes. They had nothing to do with one another, but everything from the evening was confused in his mind. He just wanted things to work out.

He couldn't stop thinking about her as he lay in his bed. The fall of her hair, the way she smelled when she leaned in close and crushed her lips to his. He'd felt the curve of her body, so much possibility pressing into him.

He rolled over and groaned. God, he was so hard, and all he'd done was kiss her. And even then barely, in the parking lot, not even a peck in the car, such a tease when what he wanted was *more*.

What was she doing right now? Was she lying there peacefully, no thoughts of what they could be doing tormenting her sleep? Was she up, too, tossing and turning like he was? The thought made his breath catch, the fantasy that she might be as twisted in longing as he was, might need to bring her hand where he longed to press his own...

He slid down his boxers, cupped his balls in one hand, and wrapped his other fist around his shaft. The images in his mind weren't even fully formed. They came in fragments from the day—her smile, the way her eyes lit up in the sun, the snow in her lashes that night. And over and over again, the memory of her breasts pressed against his chest in the parking lot. Her foot sliding up the inside of his calf under the table, sending electricity straight to his cock.

He worked his hand up and down, his legs clenching, eyes squeezed shut. He came quickly, with a gasp as though surprised by what his mind, and his body, had done.

It was just a fantasy—she hadn't even invited him in.

And yet it didn't feel like a fantasy, something that heated him up and then, when he was done, faded away. Even after he'd cleaned up and rolled over, he still couldn't sleep. For the first time since he'd moved here, he wished he were up at the Cascade and not home alone with his dog.

Chapter Seven

Austin awoke to a world turned white, a perfect layer clinging to the trees. As soon as he opened the back door, Chloe went charging, rolling around in the fluff. It clung to her black and copper fur, stinging her nose as she tried to lick it off. He checked her paws to wipe ice from the pads and set her loose in the woods.

It must have stopped snowing shortly after dawn, but the clouds were low. Cloudy days in the winter were always warmer than clear, and he sweat as he jogged, Chloe nipping at her heels. When they came in, he fed her and changed into his ski clothes. The phone rang when he was halfway out the door and he tensed, expecting it to be the Kane offices again. But they didn't leave a message. Probably a telemarketer.

Austin had the first shift of ski patrol. Usually he liked to arrive early to get in a few warm-up runs. But he found himself taking the long route to the Cascade and parking at the lift closest to the hotel. He looked around the lobby, the base lodge, the bottom of the lift. He checked his cell phone. Of course he'd remembered it today. He'd even turned the ringer up and slept with it on his nightstand. It was a terrible idea—he'd probably wind up no longer interested as soon as Sam started to get close. But he couldn't stop thinking about her.

Why hadn't she called? Didn't she need her car? It was possible she wasn't awake, but that seemed less and less likely as the morning wore on. He kept his eyes peeled for her as he combed the mountain, checking to make sure people were skiing and riding safely, answering any calls that came in over the walkie-talkie clipped to his belt.

But in the end it was she who found him, rushing up so fast she nearly crashed into him at the base of the lift as he was about to get back on.

"I can't keep up with you," she panted.

Austin lifted his goggles to see her better. Her eyes were bright, cheeks red from the wind.

"I mean, hi," she said. "Fancy meeting you here."

Austin laughed. "You were following me?"

Sam gestured up the slope. "I tried to catch you on the last two runs."

"You should've called! I was looking for you, too."

"Really?"

"Yes, really." He cocked his head. "Why didn't you call if you wanted to find me?"

"I didn't think you'd actually have your phone on you."

He pulled off a glove and unzipped his jacket pocket. "Ta-da." He pulled out his old flip phone, cracked across the top.

"I haven't seen one of those in—"

"Six years?" he offered. "Seven? Eight?"

"More like a century."

"Well, I brought it."

"Just for me?"

"What if you needed a ride to your car?"

"Aren't you supposed to be working now?" She nodded

toward his jacket, red with a white cross on the breast. "You couldn't leave even if I was desperate to make my escape."

"It's a quiet morning. No one's managed to crack their coconut yet. And you don't look very desperate."

"I just bombed down a double black diamond at the speed of light," she said. "Do with that what you will."

"Oh, shit, I came down Double Trouble, didn't I?"

"At the speed of light," she reminded him.

"Had I known I had a tail—"

"You might have made more than two turns on the entire run?"

"Are you telling me you can't keep up?"

He was rewarded by a flash of determination in her eyes, the same look Amelia got when he issued a challenge on a trail.

"I caught you, didn't I?" she said triumphantly.

He had to admit that yes, she hadn't let him stay ahead for long. It impressed him, actually. He'd been skiing fast, trying to outrun the feeling that had been building up inside him ever since he'd watched her walk out of the lodge with her hot cocoa and kicked himself for letting the moment go. It was even worse after he'd felt her lips and the press of her body against his, and then sat there as she slammed the door to his truck and went into the hotel alone.

It was a feeling like he couldn't stand to be inside his own skin, knowing there was something he wanted but couldn't seem to have. He longed to grab her and pull her close, something animal inside him that needed to hold her, kiss her, know her body against his. For a moment he could be whole.

The feeling was dangerous. It made him go too fast, push too long, lose himself on the trail. There was always a backlash, a price to pay. He could fall in too deep, get too close to the flame, and then there'd be no option but to save himself and run.

Sam cocked her head at him, eyeing him intently. "What's going through that head of yours?" she asked.

"I'm thinking that I don't usually get to ask a beautiful woman if she'd like to ride in a chairlift with me. It's a whole new kind of nervous." He realized as he said it that, in a way, that was exactly what he'd been thinking. How to be next to her without getting too close.

"I'm here, aren't I?" she said. "Don't tell me I risked life and limb on Double Death—"

"Double Trouble," he laughed.

"Just to walk away empty-handed."

Austin transferred his poles to one hand and extended the other, elbow bent, as though he were a gentleman in a topcoat inviting her in to a ball. "Shall we?" he asked.

Sam slipped her arm through his. They half skated, half hobbled to the lift, laughing at how impossible it was to ski that way, their strides mismatched, checking each other in the hip any time they tried to move. The lift operator stared at them, but that just made them laugh harder, joking about taking their show on the road. It was hard to believe he could feel this comfortable, even as a voice inside warned him not to get caught up.

And if he needed to remind himself why, here was the evidence. They'd barely gotten airborne before Sam looked over and commented, "That's some pair of gloves. Are those holes under that duct tape, or is that a style thing?"

"These?" He turned the palms over so the worst parts were hidden. "I've had them forever. Why throw them out?"

"I'm going to take that to mean holes," Sam said.

He shrugged. "They're comfortable, keep my hands warm, I don't have to worry about losing them—"

"And you definitely don't have to worry about them being stolen."

"All part of my signature look." He laughed, making

it into a joke. How could he explain to someone he barely
knew how much a ratty pair of ski gloves meant to him? The
attachment was silly, he knew. And yet he couldn't let it go.

His uncle had given Austin the gloves when he was
accepted onto the U.S. Ski Team. After everything that
happened with his father, the hammer, and his busted knee,
those gloves reminded him somebody cared. It was pretty
pathetic, and he knew Sam would think he was sentimental
and crazy if he told her. Hell, it was what he thought of himself
sometimes.

But his effort to get her laughing worked. She pressed her
leg close to his, their skis overlapping. "You have a signature
look?"

"Isn't that how you found me on the mountain? You said,
'There goes that handsome devil with the duct tape on his
gloves—I'd recognize him anywhere!'"

"Actually, I couldn't see your gloves from up top. I was
pretty far away when I first started chasing you down."

He swiveled as best he could to face her. "How'd you
know it was me?"

He thought he saw her blush, but maybe it was the flush
from being outside. "It's the way you ski. I could spot you
from a mile away."

"You haven't even seen me ski," he said, confused.

Now she was definitely blushing. "I saw you ski yesterday."

"That was like two seconds, when we were coming down
after Amelia's run."

Sam shook her head. "I watched you ski before that.
Didn't you think it was weird that I happened to be there
right when Amelia fell?"

Austin thought it over. He hadn't noticed her until she
stopped to help Amelia, and even then, he didn't give her
any thought until she lifted her goggles and suddenly she
was there, present, a force in his life in ways he still couldn't

understand.

"I just thought you were skiing down and happened to come over and help," he said carefully.

"I did. But there's a reason I was right behind you guys. I was watching your lesson." She paused. "Actually I was afraid you were going to think I was annoying, hanging around and listening in."

"I'm sorry, I get kind of focused during these things. I don't really notice anyone else," he admitted.

"I'm glad I wasn't creepy stalker lady, then."

"I hate to break it to you, but your creepiness needs some work, if that's what you're going for."

She laughed. "That's a relief. I saw you guys do a few runs, and the thing where you had them ski without poles?" She looked at him so intently that he wanted to turn away, except he couldn't, because the brown in her eyes was flecked with gold just like her hair when it caught the sun. He wondered if it was possible to kiss someone when you were both wearing helmets, goggles up over your head, or whether you'd wind up mashing your faces together and wish you hadn't tried.

"You were beautiful," Sam was saying, and it shocked Austin out of his reverie. "When you skied, the way you turned, how you moved your arms—you looked like you were flying over the snow."

"That's what I wanted them to feel. When they're racing, sometimes they forget the basic turns, the simple things to do with their weight. And they forget, too, what it feels like when they're in it, when everything is exactly right and you just go."

"I saw that. I still see it when you ski. When you were coming down Double Death—"

"Trouble." Austin laughed.

"Death," Sam insisted again. "You still looked like that. There's something so distinctive about the way you move, I knew it was you right away. Too bad I started chasing after you before I saw the double black sign."

"You must have done okay on it."

"Sure, but I'm a little rusty. That whole over-three-years-since-I've-last-been-on-skis thing isn't helping my game."

"It's just like riding a bike," Austin offered.

"That's what I told myself. Except it isn't." She paused. "It's like walking. Like breathing. The kind of thing you instinctively know how to do."

The top of the lift was coming up, but Austin wished it weren't. He would have been perfectly happy to ride the lift all the way back down if it meant he got to keep talking to Sam, looking out at the trees covered in snow, the clouds lifting overhead to reveal the white peaks all around.

She might not have jumped to defend him against the Kanes, but she got it. She understood what mattered about being here. If he'd woken up that morning wondering what to do if and when Steven Park called again, being here with Sam only strengthened his resolve.

"So are you supposed to be doing patrol-type things?" she asked after they glided off the lift.

"I mostly just have to ski. Keep an eye on everything unless I get word I have to be somewhere."

"Are you allowed to have someone following you, if she can keep up?"

"I was afraid you'd be too smart to ask."

Sam leaned forward on her skis. "Am I about to regret this?"

"Come on." He grinned. "Let's fly."

He took her down a single black first, a warm-up to get them used to each other. He skied first, then let her get ahead so he could watch. He knew she'd be decent—she carried herself with comfort even when they were standing around, and he'd seen her ski briefly with Amelia. But he couldn't help smiling as they hit their stride, turning side by side, weaving together down the trail. It was a kind of dance, not simply to ski on the same slope as someone but to ski *with* them, aware of their body, their turns. She was good—really good. At the bottom she flashed a grin and said, "That's all you've got?" so he opted for a steeper run, one that made a narrow chute through the trees that he always liked after it snowed, when the trees were heavy with snow and hanging low over the trail.

"Have you skied the Diamond Bowl?" he asked when they got to the bottom, breathless and windblown, Sam spraying snow over his skis as she pulled into a stop beside him.

She shook her head. "Too terrifying."

"I don't believe anything scares you."

She pressed her shoulders into her poles, leaning her weight forward to stretch out her calves in her boots. "Trust me," she said. "There's plenty you don't see."

"Come on, let's try it."

"I'm not good at moguls."

"You're good at everything. I'll teach you."

"It's going to be embarrassing."

"For who? You?" Austin shook his head. "I've taught five-year-olds. Fifty-year-olds. I can teach anyone to ski."

"I'm afraid I'm not nearly as bendy as a ski-wee. Or as close to the ground."

"But you're not fifty," he pointed out.

"Not quite."

"Something tells me that if I make it a challenge, you'll be the first one bombing down."

Sam stabbed the snow with a pole. "You're not supposed to have me pegged this easily."

"So we're on?"

"Shit," Sam said, shaking her head. "We're on."

Chapter Eight

The bowl was exactly what it sounded like, a scoop hollowed out of the side of the mountain. It dropped down from a craggy ridge that ran in a jagged line up to the highest point. A few trees dotted the trail, but for the most part it was open, less a set trail than a windswept, treeless expanse.

This wasn't an ordinary steep run, the kind where Sam knew to bend her knees and tighten her turns, and she would make it down. As if the bowl wasn't hard enough on its own, the entire thing was a mogul field dotted with giant, snowy bumps. It was a different kind of skiing and to Sam, infinitely harder.

Sam had spent the better part of that morning staring at her phone, debating what to do. It wasn't true what she'd told Austin. She'd known he'd pick up for her—or rather, for the person he thought she was. But even with the timeline she'd promised Steven, the threat of an anxious board, and emails from the Hendersons' lawyers hounding them to finish the sale, she couldn't bring herself to do it.

She'd told herself she was only skiing a few quick runs

as long as she was here. But she'd been looking at every ski patrol jacket she saw. Of course she'd been looking for him.

Her father never would have jeopardized a deal like this. He never would have delayed a signing or given the board reason to doubt him.

But now was *not* the time to turn to Austin and say, *By the way, I'm Samantha Kane, and I'm going to bring the full wrath of my billion-dollar company down on you if you don't sign over half the land you clearly love*. Now was the time to make sure she didn't throw up from sheer terror as she looked at the drop they were about to ski down.

"Nervous?" Austin asked with a grin as the chairlift carried them up.

"You'd better wipe that smile off your face before I knock it off," Sam grumbled, but that just made him laugh.

"Success," he boasted.

She raised an eyebrow.

"I found a way to get under your skin," he explained.

"That's your goal?" she asked.

"Well, no. Not when you put it like that." He bit his lip, no longer looking quite so gleeful. "You're just so put together," he finally said. "So calm." He smiled. "I like it."

"You're the unflappable one," Sam countered. "Oh, look, my prized skier is bleeding all over the trail. No biggie, let's go finish the run."

"I was trying not to escalate!"

"Which proves my point. Unflappable."

Austin nudged his leg against hers in the narrow chair. She shoved him back as best as she could, even though it was like pushing a rock. At least his teasing helped take her mind off how much worse the bowl looked the higher they rose.

She swiveled to look behind them at the height they'd climbed. It was a rookie mistake. Her stomach dropped at the sight.

"You can do this, Sam. You're the boss." Austin put a hand on her knee, and Sam almost gasped out loud. *Now* was when he decided to tell her he knew what she was hiding?

But he flashed a grin and she realized it was just an expression, a way to pump her up before the big run.

There was no way he'd be here like this, touching her leg, grinning at her, if he so much as suspected who she was. The thought was reassuring—her secret was safe.

Too bad his trust made her feel even worse.

But he was right, wasn't he? She *was* the boss. Whether she wanted it or not, this was her show. "Damn straight," she murmured, adjusting her gear over her face as they got to the top.

"That's my girl," Austin said and pushed off quickly from the lift, making her scramble to catch up, because what the hell did it mean that she was *his girl* when all they'd done was kiss? She had to stop this, she had to come clean, she couldn't take another second before she—

But then she was standing over the edge of the bowl, and all the words leaked from her brain.

"Don't look at the sign," Austin instructed.

"What sign?" Sam asked, whirling around to see what she'd missed.

"Don't," he repeated, using his pole to nudge her away. But it was too late—she'd seen. Maybe not the whole thing, but the words "caution" and "catastrophic" had a way of jumping out.

"Austin," she pleaded.

"Don't even think about telling me you can't."

"Are you this mean to your students? Because if I'm the boss then I'm firing your ass."

He slid slowly down along the long spine that ran from the top of the chairlift over the lip of the bowl, but he kept his eyes on her. "I'll do something to your ass, too."

Hidden by her face mask, Sam's jaw dropped. "What did you say?"

He shrugged. "Guess you'd better come and find out."

"You are one dirty bastard," she accused, but it worked. It got her to push off from where she'd been standing, paralyzed, and follow him along the ridge.

When Sam stopped beside him, he grabbed her waist and drew her near, their skis overlapping, his hips pressing close enough to make her heart pound from something other than fear. He leaned in, his lips next to her face, whispering as another skier whizzed past, "Oh, sweetheart. You have no idea."

By now Sam's heart was banging in her chest. She couldn't remember the last time someone had ripped the words away from her like this. She knew this was a bad idea. She knew the closer she got the more it would come crumbling down.

She just needed a little more time—a night to get him out of her system so she could screw her head back on and get back to work.

Provided she could make it down this trail first. The top of the bowl was the hardest part, nothing but a clear drop away from the line where they stood. She looked for an escape route, some safer trail snaking out to the side. But Austin, seeming to read her mind, said, "There's no getting away," and she wondered if he was talking about the trail or something else altogether.

"Your dad didn't take you up here?" he asked as they gazed down.

Sam shook her head, her mouth too dry to speak.

"It's a shame. Look how beautiful it is."

It was a reminder to Sam to look up, and when she did she was once more at a loss for words—but this time not because of terror or lust. The whole mountain stretched out at their feet, an endless expanse of snow and trees down to the valley below.

"It's something else up here," she murmured.

"Worth it for the view alone."

"Unless it's the last thing I ever see."

"Would I let anything happen to you?"

"I don't know," Sam said truthfully. "I barely even know you."

Austin leaned in to her again. "Yes, you do," he whispered.

He was so close, kissably close, but Sam made herself concentrate on the trail. She couldn't say yes to him, no matter how true it felt. Because he *didn't* know her. And if he did—or *when* he did…well, she didn't know what he'd do. She only knew it was going to be bad.

Her stomach knotted in a way that made her nerves from the ride up feel like nothing. Fear of the trail could be overcome. It was a boardroom, a speech, the day she officially became CEO. Her nerves rattled until it was over, and then it hardly seemed worth worrying about anymore.

This feeling with Austin was different. She pushed it down, hard, as small as it would go.

"Are we doing this or what?" she said.

He pushed over the edge so suddenly Sam wanted to yell for him to wait—she was kidding, she wasn't ready, she couldn't actually take this on by herself. But before she knew it he was down below, and she couldn't wait another second on the rim by herself. Because if she didn't do it now she never would, and there'd be no hope of anything further with Austin, because unbelievably hot Olympic-caliber athletes didn't take home women and fuck them senseless if they had to be escorted down by ski patrol because they were too chickenshit to tackle the trail.

Plus, he *was* ski patrol. Which meant he'd be the one to save her, and he was already too far down to come back.

She clenched her jaw like when she was little, afraid to

jump off the pier into Lake Washington on the hottest days of summer. Doing it anyway because she didn't want to be left behind when her father jumped first. The thought of him sent a jolt through her heart, and then she was moving even though she didn't remember giving her legs permission to go.

The first turn was sheer terror, weightlessness rising up in her stomach as the ground dropped away.

And then her skis found their purchase and suddenly she remembered how to do this. One turn led to another until she was past the lip of the trail and down in the thick of the moguls, and there was no going back. She was making it happen. Because she could, and because there was no other way.

She stopped next to Austin, breathless, her quads on fire even though they weren't even halfway down the trail.

"How does it feel?" he asked, grinning.

"Holy shit," she said.

"You looked good up there."

"Holy shit," she repeated.

Her legs were shaking. Her mind seemed to have gone blank except for her capacity to swear. Somewhere inside her jacket her phone buzzed, but no way was she getting it now.

"Come on," he said. "Pick a line."

She looked down at the trail and all that she still had to conquer. "I don't know," she admitted. "You go first, I'll follow."

"No, you choose. Look down below you and plan where you're going to turn. Mark where on the bumps your skis are going to hit. It should be three-quarters up, just around the side." He demonstrated with his pole where on the next mogul her feet should land. "You're getting a little stuck in the ruts. That's where it's icy and it's hard to stay in control."

"But I can't turn that fast," Sam said. "I pick up too much speed."

"That means you need to whip the turn around more before you go on to the next." He bounced on his skis, facing sideways across the mountain. "Each time you bring your skis around, stay perpendicular to the drop. You can take the turns as slow as you want—you're in control."

"I always am," she said pointedly.

"You're in control, as long as you let the mountain take you just a little."

"I can be taken, too."

He let out a low groan. "I like the sound of that."

"You go first. I want to see you," she said, afraid to get too far off topic while she was still in the middle of this, heart pounding, exhilaration making her shake.

"Okay," Austin said. "But don't just follow my line. See the turns for yourself. Visualize what you're going to do."

Sam swallowed hard. Of course she could visualize what she was going to do…to him. But she nodded. She had to focus.

Austin pushed off on his poles and jumped—he didn't ski but literally jumped down to the next bump, twisting his body and whipping his skis in the air. The accuracy was unreal. It was as though his legs were made of springs.

"Facing sideways," he called up to her. "Not picking up any speed."

"If you think I can do that you're crazy."

"I think you can do just about anything. And I'm pretty sure you know I'm right."

He took off before she could answer, and she was once again swept up by the beauty of his body and what it could do. He took the bumps so quickly and with such precision her eyes were glued on his form, trying to memorize every move. When he skied down a ways and stopped to look up at her, she didn't let herself fall prey to any more waiting. She pushed off and went.

It wasn't the same as him—she knew she didn't look like that. But she could feel the difference, the bumps falling into place so that she was skiing them instead of letting them push her around. Thank God yoga was the one thing that had kept her mind clear during the long stretch during and after her father's death. She was stronger and more flexible than she'd thought. She was grateful to her legs for not betraying her in front of this man who watched as though he could see all the way through her. Not only to where her weight shifted and her limbs bent but to something deeper, so she wasn't even sure what he was looking at when he caught her eyes.

She paused where he stood, and then they skied down together, riding the moguls, Sam trying to keep up even as she knew he was slowing down just for her. Her breath came fast, her heart racing. A bead of sweat trickled down her back.

"Don't stop," Austin urged, and she pushed harder, the trail beginning to flatten toward the bottom of the bowl but the bumps getting bigger where snow had gathered as it slid down the hill. But she was in it, she was soaring, she'd never skied like this before.

The next thing she knew she was flying, only her skis were no longer attached. For one brief airborne second her stomach jolted up to her throat and she wished everything would stop. And then she landed facedown with a mouthful of snow.

Austin pulled to an immediate stop. "Sam?"

She raised her head and gave a grunt.

"Please tell me you're alive."

She rolled onto her back and looked up at him. "Good thing I landed on a fluffy part," she groaned.

Austin popped out of his skis, went to gather hers, and brought them over. "Not hurt?" he asked.

Sam did a mental check of her body. Arms, legs, back, head. A little soreness on her butt, but he didn't need to know that. "Just my ego," she finally said.

Anyone watching from above would have seen someone from ski patrol helping a woman who had fallen. But Sam knew what else was going on. Austin's hand reached for her, but his eyes said he wanted to push her back down. And climb on top.

He held her a moment too long as she stood, then helped her brush snow from her jacket—not quite how she'd pictured his hands on her when he'd told her to visualize.

"There's nothing to be ashamed of," he said.

"I don't see you falling," she said, knocking one boot against the other to get the snow out of the bottom so she could pop it back in her binding.

Austin laughed as he put on his skis. "You think I've never fallen before?"

"I bet it's been a while."

She expected him to keep laughing, his whole "you're not hurt, get back on the horse" routine, but instead the smile dropped away and she thought she saw something new, a trace of sadness flickering over his face.

"I don't have an opportunity to push myself as much as I used to," he said.

Sam didn't know how to respond. Because the Diamond Bowl wasn't hard for him? Because he was no longer competitive like he once was?

But just as quickly he brightened again and so, like him, she decided not to push it. It wasn't like she wanted to get personal. The more she learned about him, the more he'd ask about her. That wasn't the way to make sure she wound up in his bed.

"I'm still embarrassed," she grumbled, adjusting her jacket after her inelegant dive.

"Falling lets you know you're doing it right."

Sam screwed up her face. "I know you're the expert, but

I'm pretty sure falling means you're doing it wrong."

"Falling means you're pushing yourself, making yourself get better. If you're not falling, you're complacent. You've stopped growing. And what's the point?"

Sam forgot the promise she'd just made to keep things light. "Are you complacent? Have you stopped growing since you no longer fall?"

He took a breath, then seemed to think better of answering. She was afraid she'd blown it by taking things too far. Finally he said, "This isn't something I can keep getting better at anymore. My knee's not good enough to support me like it used to. I can ski all over this mountain, but there's a limit, and I know what it is. Any time I forget, the pins keeping me together remind me I'm not nineteen anymore."

He extended his left leg and knocked his pole against it. Sam pictured a massive fall, a blowout, the kind of thing you saw on the Olympics that made your heart rocket to your throat. No wonder he was so blasé about a bloody nose or a face plant into a powdery mogul, cheeks wet with snow but otherwise fine.

"You really have pins in your knee?" she asked.

"If you're lucky I'll show you," he said with a wink.

"But that means you'll have to take off your pants." She flashed him a grin. No possible way to be more direct that she wanted him naked and on top of her, underneath her, standing before her so she could admire every inch.

"You must be good at your job, able to put two and two together like that."

"Not that good," Sam murmured, wishing he hadn't had to bring up the J word just then.

"That's okay. You don't have to be too good around me."

He was so close she could feel the warmth of his breathing, his sweat from the run. It was amazing there wasn't steam coming off them from how hot they both were.

But he wasn't touching her. He wasn't kissing her. She should turn away, make this stop right now.

"You're an excellent teacher, you know that?" she said quietly, raising her eyes to meet his.

"I'm a fast learner, too." He didn't let go of her gaze.

Sam was glad they were almost down the trail, because she wasn't sure she could trust her legs to hold her up for much longer. She didn't care that it was the middle of the day, they were on a mountain bundled in a zillion layers, and that vibrating in her pocket was probably Steven wanting to know if Mr. Reede had signed. Now. She wanted him now.

"We shouldn't stand around," Austin said. "We'll get cold."

"We should get moving," she agreed.

But he didn't pull away.

"You're the leader." Sam nudged him.

"But I called you the boss."

"Not today I'm not."

"I want to show you something."

"The pins in your leg?"

"Not quite."

"Am I warm, or cold?"

"I think you know how hot you are."

Sam flushed down to her toes. "Tell me what it is."

"I'm going to take you there."

He pushed off before she could think of a clever comeback, and once again she was scrambling behind him, a trickle of snow melting down under her face mask, stinging her clavicle with the sudden cold.

Chapter Nine

They cut over to the main part of the mountain and took the chairlift to the top. Sam pestered him the whole time to find out where they were going. Austin could tell she was used to being in charge, and he loved driving her nuts with anticipation. It made her talkative. She wanted to know his favorite trail, his favorite part of the mountain, what he liked best about the area, what he would want to see changed.

"Nothing," he said when they were on the lift. "I don't want it to change."

"That's impossible," Sam argued. "Things can always get better. Couldn't there be more snowmaking? More trails? There's that whole second peak that notches above where the lift goes—what if that were open with trails?"

"You sound like a Kane," Austin said, and he meant it in a ribbing way, but Sam's mouth snapped shut. He guessed he'd made it pretty clear last night what he thought of the Kanes. He regretted sounding as though he were insulting her.

"Part of what makes Gold Mountain so beautiful is that it's *not* all trails," he tried to explain. "Isn't it nice to look up and see trees, the rocky part of the peak, and appreciate the untamed parts of this place?"

"Sure," Sam said. "But I'm not talking about making the whole resort one giant trail. I'm saying, what if more of this area were accessible? Isn't there *some* kind of change the Kanes could offer that would make you want to sell that land they want?"

He shook his head. "No way. There're no magic words that will suddenly make me want to turn my backyard into luxury condos and parking lots." He paused. "Actually, I'm surprised they haven't gotten in touch today. Did I tell you the head of the company is supposed to be in town to come after me herself? It's weird not to have heard anything. Maybe it's not going to happen."

"Maybe." Sam looked skeptical, and Austin thought he probably shouldn't be burdening her with his problems.

"If they expanded the place, then I wouldn't be able to spend the morning skiing with you when I'm supposed to be patrolling, because the mountain would be completely overrun," he said with a grin.

"I'm not trying to keep you from your job," Sam protested—although not too strongly, he noted. "I should probably do some work, too."

"Please. I'm not going to meet with those people anyway. My job is to ski. Which we're doing. And I'm not letting you get away that easily."

"So now I'm an add-on to your job, just a typical day?" Austin was afraid she was mad until he saw the teasing glint in her eyes.

He shrugged. "It's one of the perks that goes with the glamorous life of a has-been racer. Every day I pick another beautiful woman to take down the most treacherous trails."

"Well, aren't I lucky."

"You should know it's a tough job to get. You have to

have a sense of humor, be sharp as a whip, no bullshit, and last but not least, you have to actually be able to ski."

"And not fall flat on your face." Sam cringed. "I guess I blew that audition."

Austin pulled off one of his gloves and ran a finger down her cheek. A lock of hair was caught in the strap of her helmet, and he gently pulled it free. "You're not performing for me."

"We're going to get stuck on this lift," Sam murmured, not moving her eyes from his. But she was right, they were at the top, and they scrambled to get the bar up and dismount in time.

"So have I convinced you to blow off work a little longer?" he asked when they got off the lift.

"You have no idea," was all she answered, and she asked what he had planned.

Austin led them away from the area where skiers and snowboarders were dismounting. There was always a bottleneck at the top, when people suddenly turned around and were hit by the view. But Austin was only looking at one thing, and it wasn't the same sight he'd been looking at for years. "I'm pretty sure I was about to kiss you before the lift ruined my game."

"Well, then you should get back to it." Sam gave a half smile, a tantalizing mix of serious and playful that made him want to pounce.

But he resisted, even though it was hard to care that there were people around, and the attendant who watched the top of the lift, and he was in his official ski patrol gear.

Not that what he was planning was much more professional. "Come on," he said, pushing off on his skis. "I told you I was taking you somewhere."

"Not even a small kiss?" she asked.

He stopped in his tracks, waiting for her to follow. "I see patience isn't your strong suit."

"Absolutely not," Sam said bluntly. Then her eyes flashed. "I get what I want."

Austin turned so his skis were splayed out, keeping him from backsliding down the slope, and planted his poles in front of him. He leaned his shoulders into the mountain, looking up at her. "Sweetheart, I have no intention of denying you a thing."

He turned and pushed off again. He didn't have to look back to know she was following. He had no doubt she'd stay beside him the whole time.

Every ski place had the equivalent of the Wanderer, a meandering trail that skirted the outer boundaries of the mountain. It was never crowded, because it was long and windy and not very steep. But after the runs they'd just done, it was nice to give their legs a break and cruise.

The trail wasn't the reason Austin had come here. It was the cutoff. He was afraid Sam was going to miss the stop since he gave her no warning, but she was right behind him. He realized she'd been skiing in his tracks, mirroring him turn for turn. The thought made him smile.

He stopped where bright ribbon strung along the trees warned skiers not to go off the trail. Austin glanced around, but they were alone. No one would see the man in the ski patrol jacket lift the rope for the woman to slide under before he followed.

"Is this your dirty little secret?" Sam asked as she crossed into the woods. "Sneaking off-duty when you're supposed to be on patrol?"

Austin patted the walkie-talkie in his pocket. "We're not going out of range."

"I take it this is a regular part of your route, then."

"I have to have a place to take the ladies when they flag me down on the trail."

Sam thwacked him with her pole, and he responded by grabbing for her waist, but she was quick and slid away. "Where are we going, anyway?"

"You said you get what you want," he said. "I do, too."

Sam made an appreciative sound. "I can't wait to find out what that means to you."

Austin felt a flush creep up his neck and pointed to a faint opening through the trees. "In the summer it's a real trail. In the winter you kind of pick your way over."

"It goes straight across?"

"Exactly. You'll know when you get there."

"My life is in your hands," Sam said matter-of-factly as she began to edge through the trees.

"It helps if you don't hit anything. Or fall."

Sam raised her pole, which he took to be an extension of her middle finger. He laughed and rushed to keep up.

And then it was just the two of them and the trees laden with snow. Austin's chest hummed with anticipation. It seemed like there was nothing but forest all around, but he knew Sam had seen it when she paused.

"That's it," he said. "Keep going."

She pulled up to the small wooden hut. Austin stopped beside her and popped out of his skis, propping his poles in a snowdrift. He looked at Sam to see whether she was ticked off that they'd come here. The whole point of skiing, after all, was to ski—not find weird little places off the trail.

But she was grinning as she took off her skis, her face mask pulled below her chin to let the wind cool her after pushing through the trees. "Thank you," she said quietly, and he knew she felt it, the steady tug that kept calling him to this place even though the trails were elsewhere, and the lifts, and the rest of his life.

He pulled off his helmet and dropped it on the platform of the shelter, raised a few feet above the ground. Sam did the same. Her hair was in a side braid over her shoulder, long strands of it loose around her face. He felt himself stirring at her red cheeks, red lips, the way she laughed, loose and limber. The way she came undone.

He couldn't wait any longer. He kissed her the way he'd been wanting to ever since she'd called his name that morning. Ever since she pulled her lips from his in the parking lot just as he'd been about to go in for more. That had been one thing, thrilling in its own right. But this was something else altogether.

This was the kiss he'd been thinking about all night, craving all morning, and now he couldn't hold back. And it seemed she couldn't, either, because she kissed him with the same intensity, running her hands up his chest, around his neck.

It didn't matter that she didn't live here, that a relationship was out of the question. It was probably *because* a relationship wouldn't happen that he could let himself get this close. He wrapped his arms tighter around her as though this were all that existed in the world. Just the two of them, the mountain, the clean winter air. The taste of her tongue on his lips.

Austin pulled off a glove and slid his bare hand up under her jacket, around her waist, eliminating at least that one barrier between them. She let out a low moan as he pulled her closer. The feel of her hips, the arch of her back, gave more than a hint as to what was to come.

Sam unzipped the front of his jacket, but there were too many layers between them. Taking her hand, he climbed onto the platform and hoisted her up after him.

The shelter had three walls. The fourth side was an open space facing out. The wood was worn and knotted, the roof slanted steeply and heavy with snow. "What is this place?"

Sam asked.

"There are old mining shacks all over the far side of the mountain. They took out most of them when it became a ski resort, but a few markers remain. This one must have been a shelter. People still use it in the summer, when they hike to the top."

"Pretty quiet in the wintertime, though."

"Nobody comes here," he whispered. He was already tugging her toward him.

Sam latched on tight to the front of his ski pants. He couldn't hold back his groan. God, he wanted this. He wanted her. He pressed her to the back wall of the shelter, away from the wind. Protected from the elements it was quiet, nothing but the gasp of their breathing quickening as Sam's teeth grazed his bottom lip.

It was too cold to take their jackets off all the way, but they were unzipped and Austin slid his hand under her sweater to her breasts. He tweaked her nipple between his forefinger and thumb and was rewarded with a low moan in his ear. He pushed her more firmly against the smoothed, worn logs of the old wall.

"Is this what you want?" he whispered, his lips grazing her ear.

"Please," she whimpered. She spread her legs, her back against the wall. Austin lifted her hands over her head and held them there as he crushed his lips to hers.

She arched her back, pressing forward. He teased her for a moment, keeping his body just out of reach, making her plead for what he wouldn't let her have. And then when the frenzy seemed too much to bear, he ground his whole body against her, pinning her to the wall with his arms, his chest, his hips. His cock pushed against the front of his pants, and he knew she could feel how hard he was. She shifted her hips, rearranging her position so he was hitting her right at the soft cleft between her legs.

He was drilling into her, rubbing right where she wanted it. Her head leaned back and hit the wall. She clung to his shoulders, thrusting her hips in time with his.

"Austin." She said his name like a breath. "I don't have a condom."

Dammit, he didn't, either. This wasn't exactly a typical workday for him.

"I can still fuck you," he said.

"No." She shook her head. "I mean it."

Austin unbuttoned her ski pants all the way and slid his hand down the front. His fingers danced over her panties, feeling the warmth that radiated there. She was damp through the cloth. Gently he slid the fabric to the side.

"I can still fuck you," he whispered again, slipping a finger inside her and running it along her silken skin.

Her lips parted, a single exhalation. Her legs opened farther, inviting. Demanding. He slid another finger inside.

She was so wet. So, so wet, like a dream. He moved slowly, letting the movement of her hips set the pace. He slid his fingers in and out, gliding over the eager bud of her clit and then plunging inside her again, circling the place he knew she was yearning for and then keeping his fingers dancing on the spot. Sam's legs jerked. She threw her head back. Austin would have thought he'd give anything to replace his fingers with his cock, but the way she cried out in ecstasy, he had to change his mind. He wouldn't replace this moment for anything, not with the pleasure coursing through her.

But Sam, apparently, had other things in mind. She unzipped his pants, straining for him even as she couldn't stop grinding against his hand. She tightened with desire as she pulled his cock free and started stroking. All of him throbbed at her touch.

"Use my wetness," she said, her hand working over him.

He pulled his fingers from her slowly, already missing her warmth. He wasn't sure what she wanted, but then she slid her own hand under her panties—the fabric impossibly soft, hugging her hip bones so all he wanted was to place his tongue there and bite her delicate flesh—and skimmed her fingers over his shaft.

"Shit," he groaned, rolling his head back, closing his eyes.

"You did that to me," she murmured, repeating the movement.

Her fly was open, her pants scrunched partway down. Austin put his hands firmly on the fabric around her hips and yanked down to expose what he wanted. He dropped to his knees on the wood floor. He had to feel her. He had to taste her. He couldn't stay away.

The floor was cold, but he had his ski pants on, padding for his knees. He reached up and pushed her hips back so she was locked against the wall.

"Austin," she began, but the word ended in a moan as his tongue found her clit. She shifted, widening her stance to give him access. On his knees, feeling her guide him, he dragged his tongue along the length of her slit, licking slow and deep and then circling faster, until she was panting and crying his name.

Her pelvis thrust forward, her back arched. He could feel her strain, as though she wanted to lift her legs, but the ski boots kept her anchored in place. It was ridiculous to be outside in the middle of winter like this, in the shelter where he'd spent countless hours just thinking, alone. But the surprise of it, the stolen moment, the fact that he was still in his ski patrol jacket made the whole thing so unbearably hot he reached for his cock and jacked himself as he worked vigorously on her clit.

She must have been able to tell, because her hands grabbed fistfuls of his hair and tugged. He let go of his cock and reached up to caress her thighs, her hips, the curve of her stomach, feeling under her sweater up to her breasts. Shit, she was incredible.

"Austin," she said. Never had he heard his name like that, spoken as a pant, a need. She whispered it again, like a chant, pulling his face toward her and grinding into him. He ran his hands along her thighs. A faint yes escaped her lips. His thumb teased around her folds.

When he thought from her moans that she was going to burst open from the seams, he slid a finger inside her, then another, while he sucked on her clit. A few strokes like this and he felt her thighs vibrating, literally vibrating on either side of his face. He circled her G-spot with his fingers, circled her clit with his tongue. Her thighs clamped so tight around him there was nothing in his world except the heat from her skin and the sweet, soft taste of her coming on his tongue.

He licked her slowly, drawing out her orgasm. When he took his fingers from her, she shuddered. She kept her hands on his hair, his neck, his shoulders, his back, refusing to break contact as he stood. He licked clean the fingers that had been inside her, then ran his hand down the scruff of his beard.

"I'm assuming you came?" he said quietly, cupping her jaw in his palm.

She pretended to push him away, but it was as though she didn't have the strength in her limbs to go through with it. Or that on second thought, she didn't want him even an arm's length away. "Don't pretend that you didn't know." She smiled a dreamy grin, pure bliss on her face. She was so gorgeous, when she touched his cock he thought he was going to shoot right there on the spot.

She stroked him, getting to know him, running her thumb over the swollen tip. A groan in the back of her throat—he hoped that meant appreciation. She was just trying to warm him up, but she didn't understand. Going down on her had been pure pleasure for him. When she began lowering to her knees, her fist was tight, pumping, and just the thought of those lips on his dick was enough to make his eyes squeeze shut.

"I'm too close," he gasped, grabbing her shoulder to stop her. "I'm going to—"

He couldn't even say the words.

Sam let her palm glide along the underside of his shaft. She worked her hand over the tip and slid down again, pumping him firmer and faster as his hips began to buck. She was leaning back against the wall and he tilted forward, one hand up over her shoulder, bracing himself against the wall. He could feel the tightening in his balls, the electric energy slinging all the way from his spine to his toes.

Sam's jacket had slid partway off her shoulders. She used her spare hand to lift her shirt, exposing her stomach to him. She pulled him so the tip of his cock grazed her skin, soft and warm. A cry caught in Austin's throat. The sight of him in her hand, moving, thrusting. His cock heavy and thick against the smooth line from her belly button down to the thin fabric of her panties, her pants still unzipped and partway down, the indecency of it even more erotic than if she'd been undressed. The hint of the curl of dark hair where he'd buried his tongue.

Urgently, he tugged her shirt up higher, exposing her to him. The underside of her bra, the swell of her breasts. She'd come in his mouth and he hadn't even seen her breasts.

"Come on me," she breathed.

"Oh, fuck." Austin groaned. Did she know how dangerous she was?

"I want you to come all over me."

As if she knew that was all it would take.

The heat of her fist, the slide of his cock on her skin. He came on her while she pumped him until he had given everything to her. And then she stood there, pants unzipped, shirt yanked up, his come all over her stomach, enjoyment all over her face.

"Shit." He shook his head, embarrassment heating his cheeks. "I wasn't going to last."

His cock was still out, still hard. He held it, feeling the pulse lingering inside him. His balls ached, as though what he'd had was just the beginning. As though there might never be enough.

Sam's eyes were fixated on his cock in his fist. Slowly she lowered herself to the ground in front of him. This time he didn't object.

"I just want to taste you," she murmured. He moved his fist away and let her take him in her mouth. She sucked him slowly, running her tongue along the underside of his shaft, flicking at his balls, swirling over the tip. Cleaning the last drops from him.

He liked it, this slow, sensual play. The idea that she wanted him in her mouth because she wanted him in her mouth—not because she had to, or was only reciprocating, or because it was some expected way to get him off.

He ran his fingers lightly through her hair. His eyes were closed when a crackle came from his pocket.

"Shit, my walkie-talkie." He fumbled to unclip it.

"I'm heading over to the Basin and then turning in," came the staticky voice.

"Copy that," Austin choked, his breath all over the place. "I'm finishing up my last round."

Sam flicked her tongue over his balls. Austin tried to cover his gasp with a cough. She looked up with a satisfied grin. If she liked him flustered, she was clearly in luck.

"All clear?" the voice asked.

"No noise."

"Haven't seen you. Asked around at the patrol hut, but no one said you'd popped in."

Austin gripped the walkie-talkie in one hand as he tried

to stuff himself back in his pants. Sam stood, one eyebrow raised, waiting to see how he was going to talk himself out of this one.

"I got a report of some kids that ducked into the woods off Wanderer," Austin said quickly. "I'm just coming out of there now." Sam giggled, then covered her mouth when he flapped his hand at her.

"Any sign of 'em?"

"Nah, I'm heading in."

"Okay, catch you back at the hut. Tell next shift to keep an eye open."

"I'm sure it's fine. I'll let you know if anything comes up."

"Roger that."

"Later."

Austin put the walkie-talkie back in his pocket, heart pounding in his chest. He shook his head at Sam, trying to get his clothes back where they were supposed to be.

"Kids in the woods?" Sam shook her head. "You'd better keep an eye on them. Wouldn't want anyone getting into trouble."

Austin rolled his head from side to side, stretching out his neck. "I think it's a little late for that."

Sam used a tissue to clean up her stomach, but it was by no means a perfect job. When she put her clothes back in place, that secret was still underneath. Austin knew he was late, but he couldn't turn away, his eyes wide. She came closer to him, her voice low, fingertips trailing up and down his chest.

"Here's what's going to happen. You're going to go be mister ski patrol hero with your buddies. Meanwhile, I'm going to ski down with your come all over me. I'm going to feel you every second of the day." She bit his lip. "And nobody's going to know."

She tried to pull away, a tease, but he grabbed her wrist with one hand and her ass with the other, pressing her hard against his hips. He held her in a real kiss, a proper kiss, the taste of her still on his lips. How could he go back to work like this, knowing she was out there covered with him, the memory of her on his fingers, all over his chin? He had to get back to the main part of the mountain, act like he'd actually been working for the last—how long had they been up here? He had to clean up before practice, that was for sure.

"I want you to be thinking about me," he said, his voice low, still gripping her tight.

"I could say the same thing to you. I know how you get out there, all focused on the team."

He shook his head. "Doesn't mean there isn't room for thoughts of you."

"I want you to be thinking about how you're going to fuck me," she whispered. "And while that was good—" She took his hand and brought it between her thighs. "You know what I mean. You know what I want."

"Does this mean there's a next time?" he asked, rubbing his fingers over her crotch, wanting to slide his fingers down there and feel her heat again. He was surprised she was so eager, after her uncertainty last night. But it didn't matter. He felt it, too.

"Please tell me you're free tonight," she said.

"Normally I would be, but I've got this gorgeous woman coming over. I came on her this afternoon, you wouldn't believe how hot it was. Right on her stomach." He flicked his finger under the hem of her sweater.

Sam frowned. "I don't know about that. She sounds kind of dirty."

Austin traced the line above her ski pants. "I like dirty." He leaned close, his lips hovering just above hers.

Sam tugged on his jacket, pressing herself against him. Damn, if she could come again he would probably die of pleasure.

But he was late, he was really fucking late, and if someone happened to ski down looking for him and saw him come out of the backwoods with a woman who practically glowed with pleasure... Well, they'd know the only two kids in the woods weren't kids at all.

Reluctantly Austin pulled away and started zipping everything up. Sam, understanding, followed suit, getting her helmet and face mask together. When Austin reached for his gloves, Sam let out a laugh.

"Those things are even older than your cell phone," she said, finding her mittens on the floor. "What are they, a hundred? A hundred and fifty years old?"

"Nice." He smirked. "Try a mere fourteen."

"Fourteen-year-old gloves? That's awfully specific. Why even keep them that long?"

And in case he started thinking there was something growing here, here it was: the reminder of why he shouldn't move so fast. Because the words stung. The way she asked, it was like she was laughing at him. He could feel himself clamming up already.

"I already told you, it's the magic of duct tape. No need to get rid of them when they work fine."

"That's what I'm going to need to keep me together once you're through with me."

Austin raised an eyebrow.

"The skiing," Sam shot back. "I was talking about the skiing!"

"Funny," Austin said, wrapping her in his arms once more. "I was thinking of all the other things I'm going to do with you. None of which have you in this." He tugged at her parka, slowly unzipping it again. He could keep this physical. He didn't have to tell her anything more.

Sam grabbed his hand. "I thought you had some place to be, Coach."

"I can be late," he murmured, his lips brushed against hers.

"Something tells me you're never late."

"That's why I get a pass today."

Sam shook her head, pushing him away. "The patrol guys will talk."

"They always talk."

"The girls on the team will talk."

"They talk even more."

"This is what happens when you get so focused on what's in front of you."

"Mmm, like Sam."

She tasted like winter itself, the cold of her lips, the warmth of her tongue. But she pushed him away and passed him his helmet.

"You lead. I'm counting on you to get me down to the trail alive."

He flashed a grin at her. "Have I let you down so far?"

"Please." Sam rolled her eyes. "It's, like, not even noon."

"Nope, almost one. That's when my shift ends. I've got to eat something before practice at two."

"One?" Sam exclaimed. She grabbed his hand and dragged him back to their skis.

"You've got somewhere to be?" he asked, confused.

"Two o'clock call."

"Work?"

"You guessed it."

He sighed as he buckled his skis. "What's the meeting about?"

He was just making conversation, but Sam looked frozen on the spot.

"Don't worry about it. I won't bug you about the details," he said, backtracking.

"Sorry, it's just that I don't really have time to get into it now." She wrapped the straps of her poles around her wrists.

"The boss will kill you if you're late?"

"More like the board. But yeah, that's the basic idea."

Austin stared at her. "I was just kidding," he said.

She shook her head. "I'm not."

It wasn't the kind of comment he could just drop. What did she do, anyway? And how could she be up here, taking time off, and still have so much to deal with? But she was in a rush, and he didn't want to get in the way. "I'll show you the shortcut back to the base. It's a quick stretch, you barely have to turn."

"You barely turn anyway," Sam accused.

"I didn't think you had a problem with being direct."

Sam glanced down at her stomach, then flashed a flirty grin. Austin groaned. He had to start skiing or else he'd be on top of her, right there in the snow, not giving a damn about the cold. Or their jobs. Or what anyone skiing by might see.

Chapter Ten

Sam stood in the shower, letting the hot water pound over her. She soaped her stomach, lingering over the plane between her belly button and her hip. Remembering the trace of him, the dirty thrill as she came in and stripped off her clothes.

She'd say she couldn't believe what she'd done in the woods, but of course she could. Believe it, want it, relive it. Crave it all over again. The rational part of her knew this had to stop. Too bad the rest of her had other ideas.

How fast had she gone from *this isn't happening* to head back, legs parted, screaming his name? He'd felt every inch of her trembling around his fingers. She'd come on his face, pressed to his tongue. Grasped him as he came on her, a gesture so deeply personal it felt almost more intimate than fucking.

She pulled on a hotel bathrobe, hair damp and messy, clothes littering the floor. Cleaned up and away from Austin's touch, her real life stared at her accusingly from the papers and blueprints scattered across her room. *This* was who she was. Not someone reckless, passionate, and free to do as she pleased, but someone endlessly scrolling through emails. She had a company to run. And, even more pressing, she had to prove herself able to do it.

She looked at herself in the bathroom mirror and tied the robe tighter around her. She didn't look very executive right now, but that was the beauty of the conference call. Nobody had to know that Fortune 500's top Woman to Watch had just wiped come off her stomach after screaming the name of a man she'd met fewer than twenty-four hours before.

Not that there was anything wrong with that, she reminded herself. Men got to shoot their load wherever they wanted and still be presidents and CEOs.

So she liked sex. So she liked it with the guy her company was pressuring with a hard sell. Was that so wrong? It didn't mean she had to tell him everything. It didn't mean she had to get derailed.

Her phone dinged, announcing it was time. She called the office and got the news from the day, the accounts they had in progress, the deals that were already set. When it was Jim's turn to give an update, he powered through with gruff formality, no indication of the twenty-plus text messages he'd left her before—at last—abruptly dropping the issue, as though if he couldn't have her, he'd pretend they'd never done anything at all.

"Where are we on the Gold Mountain deal?" a VP demanded as soon as the first items on the agenda were done.

She was sitting on her bed with the sheets pulled back, legs crossed, bathrobe gaping so she could see the swell of her breasts in the mirror over the desk across from the bed. She looked like a stranger to herself, someone whose thighs were sore from skiing, from moguls, from clenching tight as she pressed her back against a worn wooden wall. But when she spoke, she was Samantha Kane all the way.

"As Steven has informed you, I've made contact with Mr.

Reede. We'll be ironing out the details tomorrow, Friday at the very latest. I will of course keep you informed."

She meant it to sound final, but a volley of complaints rose through the phone.

"This is the best way to ensure Mr. Reede submits to the deal." She nearly choked on her word choice but powered through. "I've made more progress with him in twenty-four hours than we did in months of letters and calls."

She didn't know how she'd become this person who lied so easily, to Austin that she knew nothing of the Kane deal, to her board that she was getting that very deal done. But this was the only way to keep them from closing in on her like vultures circling their prey.

"We've received a call from the Hendersons' lawyer," Jim said. "They're threatening to find another buyer if there's any more delay."

"No one can match what we're offering," Sam said dismissively. "It's posturing. They've waited this long—they can live through another day."

"And if Mr. Reede proves as intractable as he's always been?" She could hear the wry amusement in Jim's voice. He wanted her to sweat in front of the board. He wanted to show that he could make her dance.

Sam stood and tightened the bathrobe around her. Body posture alone could change how you sounded on the phone. She used to practice for hours how to stand, how to breathe, speaking from low in her diaphragm, finding the register to make it sound natural, like nothing anyone would dream of arguing against. The hardest parts of the job worked only when they seemed effortless, when everyone was fooled.

"Mr. Reede is signing tomorrow," she repeated. "Then the completed proposal goes to the Hendersons. We've waited years for this. We can wait another day."

"What assurance do we have?" another voice piped

up, followed by a diatribe about wasting company time and money on a "wild-goose chase." "As your board, we're authorized to take a vote if we deem you unfit to—"

"I suggest you think long and hard about what you're insinuating before you finish that sentence." Sam's voice became so cold it would have terrified her had she been on the receiving end.

"If you could tell us what you're doing to get Reede to change his mind—" Jim started, like he was too ballsy—or stupid—to care what Sam had just said. She cut him off. There'd be no more questioning her professionalism in front of the team.

"I'll be on email the rest of the day and will send a memo when the sale is complete. In the meantime, we still have other accounts. I want those action items for the Trident building."

She ended the call before she could hear whatever quips and gripes came through before they fully disconnected their phones. That was how she'd first heard her nickname, one person complaining to another that the wolf was at it again.

So let them have their names. It was probably good for morale, or bonding, or whatever. The sale would come through and then they'd see.

Tomorrow. She'd spend the night with Austin, get this thing out of her system, and then she'd present him with the papers he needed to sign. As much as she hated to admit Jim was right, she did need to remember her priorities.

Still, two days of skiing wouldn't ruin anything. Some people even took vacations for multiple days! In a row! She sat back down on the bed. She was going to close her eyes for a second. Then she'd call the Hendersons to reassure them the ink on their final part of the deal would be dry by the end of the week.

The next thing she knew, it was dark in her room and the phone was vibrating in her hand. She'd fallen asleep on top of the covers, still clutching the phone, and Austin was texting her.

I picked up those things I needed, he said.

Condoms, he had condoms. Sam felt a flutter rising inside her again.

Lucky me, she wrote back.

Her phone buzzed with his response. *It's going to be a tough competition for luckiest.*

She didn't have to rack her brain for a response. *Too bad for you I always win.*

She smiled in the dark, her lids heavy, her legs even sorer than when she'd fallen asleep. Her yoga instructor would kill her if she knew how Sam had flopped into bed without stretching. The text came back right away: *7 pm. Dinner at my place. I'll pick you up. It's on.*

Perfect. He could drop her back at her car at Mack Daddy's when they were done.

The Dipper, she reminded herself quickly. Better use the proper name if by the end of the week she was going to officially own all this land, including the peak, the resort, half of Austin's property, and the restaurant.

She checked her email again, dealing with any fires that needed to be put out while flagging whatever could wait. She was just going through the motions, though, her mind entirely elsewhere. Usually getting ready for a date involved some kind of song and dance. Would they or wouldn't they? What exactly would the night entail? But Austin had specifically let her know that he had condoms. They'd left it with the promise that he was going to—*fuck her*, that's what he'd said. She felt a warm flush spread across her chest. Was it a booty call if there was dinner involved? If it was at his house? If she really, really liked him?

Could she still like him if she knew there was no potential there?

She hoped the sex would be good enough to make up for how angry he was going to be.

But she'd known from their first kiss that it would be worth it.

It already was.

Sam grabbed her hat, scarf, and gloves and put on her boots. On her way out she stopped at the small shop on the first floor of the hotel. She walked through the aisles seeing the blueprints overlaid in her mind, where the walls were going to be knocked down, the store expanded to stock gourmet prepared foods and quick meals to supplement the full grocery store that would open farther down the access road.

She lingered over a bottle of wine but wound up grabbing a chilled six-pack instead, not sure what Austin liked but remembering he'd had beer the night before. At the register she had another idea. She bundled up and walked to the main lodge at the base of the mountain. Inside was a ski store, and she found exactly what she was looking for, including a man working the floor who tried them on for her, making sure they'd fit. "Warm but breathable," he promised. "Trust me, your boyfriend will love them."

She almost corrected him, then let the comment stand. What was she going to say? *They're just for the guy I'm fucking tonight. A little thank-you for how hard he already made me come once today.* She hoped the clerk couldn't see how much she was blushing from her own thoughts.

She walked back to the hotel and waited for Austin outside, minimizing the risk of a run-in with the concierge. She wondered what his place was like inside, where his friends lived, what they thought of Austin holding out against the Kanes. Were they all out here in the woods? Did they like it? Did they long for anything else?

The thought of Connor's beet burger made her mouth

water. Whatever Kane Enterprises wound up doing with the Dipper, they were going to have to convince Connor to stay on. Maybe they'd tear it down and build something with the same kind of charm that wasn't actually falling apart. Mack could be the bartender, not just beer but a full bar, cocktails…

She was getting ahead of herself. She held the paper bag with her purchases close to her chest. Food, sex, sleep, sale. Maybe she could fit in an afternoon of skiing after everything was done. No matter what, by this time Friday she'd be driving toward the city lights, over four billion dollars' worth of land and property in her company's name.

Or maybe the order was sex, then food. When Austin pulled up, Sam almost kissed him right when she got into the truck, except the valet guys were there. He wore a black beanie loose on his head, bits of hair sticking out underneath. He smelled of soap with a hint of wood smoke. When he pulled up to his house, she knew why. Smoke rose from the chimney, a fire burning low in the fireplace. He stoked it back up and added fresh logs when they walked in.

"I should have asked you before, but are you okay with dogs?" he asked.

Before Sam could say yes, an enormous German shepherd with a glossy coat came up and stuck her wet nose to Sam's outstretched hand.

"Sorry, she's way too friendly. Give her a chance to come in, Chloe," he scolded. "Not everyone wants to be your new best friend."

Sam laughed and let Chloe sniff her. When the dog seemed satisfied, Sam reached out and ran her fingers through her fur.

"I didn't know you had a dog," Sam said, then felt silly, because even though she'd driven by his house before—which she was never going to tell him—there were a million things she didn't know about Austin. Like what he'd done after his injury. Or what he liked to do besides ski. A million things she'd never ask, because she didn't want him turning the questions on her.

"It smells great in here," she said to cover her blunder, and pulled the six-pack from the bag.

"Nice," he said. "Leave your things by the door, I'll get a bottle opener. Do you want a glass?"

"Bottle's fine," she said, pulling off her boots and hanging up her jacket.

Bachelor in the mountains could go very, very wrong. But the house, though small, was inviting. The doorway opened into a living room with comfortable furniture, a matching heather-green sofa and love seat angled around the fireplace, a television mounted above. Stairs led to a lofted bedroom—she could see the edge of the bed, and what looked like the feet of an antique wood dresser upstairs. Next to the living room was a dining area with a large round table, and behind it an open kitchen where something delicious-smelling bubbled on the stove.

She went to stand by the sliding glass doors and looked out at what she could make of the view in the dark. There was a backyard covered in snow, and then behind it, nothing but trees. There were no neighbors, no lights, no intrusions from the outside world. Hell, she could see why he was so attached.

"It's not much," Austin said, coming up with two opened beers. "But it's home."

Sam smiled as she took her beer. "It's perfect," she said. *And so are you*, she almost added, eyeing him up and down with a quick flutter in her chest. He was wearing a button-down fitted tight across his pecs, the sleeves rolled up to expose the blond hair on his arms. She wanted to sink to her knees right there and yank off his belt, feel the satisfying slide of the leather as she pulled it through the loops, drawing out his pleasure, her fun.

Instead, he gestured for her to sit on the couch. So they

were going to be polite about it. Okay. At the last minute she remembered her gift.

"I have something for you." She brought him the other package.

He eyed her uncertainly as he unfolded the bag.

"Not much of a wrapping job," she apologized.

"You weren't supposed to get me anything."

She shrugged. "I wanted to. Come on, open it." She was getting excited anticipating the look on his face, how grateful he was going to be. Men were so hard to shop for, and yet as soon as she'd had the idea, she'd known it was perfect. The best presents were the ones there was no reason for. Just a simple way to show she'd been thinking of him.

But when he reached into the bag, his face froze, his jaw tightening in a way she'd never seen before. Even before he said, "I can't accept this, Sam," she knew that somehow, without meaning to, she'd done something wrong.

"You haven't even seen what it is," she protested.

He pulled out the gloves. They were black, with leather reinforcements across the palm and not a hole in sight. Yet he was holding them as though they might poison his hands.

He cleared his throat uncomfortably. "This is really nice, Sam."

"But?"

"But I'm sorry." He shook his head and passed them over to her. "I can't."

"Try one on," she prodded. Reluctantly he slipped his hand inside. She could tell it fit perfectly, the top cinching at just the right place up his arm so the snow and the cold wouldn't get in.

"Tell me they don't feel amazing."

He sighed. "They do. They feel amazing."

"Top of the line."

"I know." He pulled the glove off and nestled it with its

mate on the back of the couch.

"I've seen how much you work when you ski. This is warm, waterproof, but it's supposed to be breathable, it'll wick the sweat away—"

"Sam," he interrupted, taking her hands in his. She shut her mouth. "This is really, really sweet of you. But these gloves cost two hundred dollars. I can't accept that kind of gift from you."

She pulled her hands away, surprised by how stung she felt. "It's my choice. I wanted to get them for you. They're yours."

"No." He pushed them toward her. "Please."

It was such as simple thing. Such a stupid thing. And yet she could feel tears spring to her eyes. She'd been so excited to see him, and the gloves felt like an extension of that. The idea that she was trying to buy him made her feel dirty. The idea that he'd rejected being bought made her feel even worse. This wasn't his property they were talking about. She'd wanted him to know that she cared.

"I'm not concerned about the money," she said.

"I get that," he said. "It seems like it's not a big deal to you."

"No, you don't get that," she shot back. "Otherwise you'd take them without making it into an issue."

She saw the surprise on his face and immediately regretted it, not just what she'd said but the tone. Her phone call with work was still inside her, leaching out.

But Austin didn't know her like that. She didn't want him to know her like that. She wanted him to think of her like Amelia did. What was that word? *Nice.* Even when she wasn't. Even when she knew she couldn't be.

"I'm sorry," she said. "I was just excited, that's all. I don't want it to be a thing. I'll take them back."

He reached for her hand again. "Thank you."

"You wear those gloves held together by duct tape and I thought…" She couldn't finish the sentence. The idea that she'd thought he'd be excited to have a new pair of gloves had obviously been way off base, but it couldn't be just about money. Most people politely protested then were happy to accept the thing they wanted but would never have bought for themselves. But Austin had been adamant. It was like he was with the land, so damn principled he couldn't imagine things another way.

She put the gloves back in the bag. If only they fit her, she would have kept them for herself.

If only she had someone else she could give them to, but that made her think of her father and how she couldn't give them to him, could no longer give him anything, and this time she couldn't stop the tears in her eyes.

"Oh, hey, hey," Austin said quickly, reaching out to wrap her in a hug. "I'm sorry, I handled that wrong. Please, don't—"

"It's okay." She shook her head, embarrassed by such vulnerability. "It's not really that. It's…I don't know. Something just popped into my mind. It still happens like that sometimes. I think I'm fine and then all of a sudden, it's like a wave that comes out of nowhere."

"Your father?" he asked.

She nodded, then pulled away from him. "Can we start over?" She dropped the bag of gloves by the door, out of view. "I brought beer. It smells delicious in here. Your place is lovely. I thought about you all afternoon."

She forced a smile, but when Austin raised his beer and clinked it against hers the smile was real and she was back, she was okay, the gloves didn't matter when she bought them and they wouldn't matter when she brought them back. Austin kissed her, the kind of kiss that said he'd been thinking about her, too. "Can I give you the grand tour?"

"Sure," she said, on solid footing now.

He turned his arm to take in the open floor plan. "This is it."

She laughed. "Fabulous. What's cooking?"

"Soup and fresh-baked bread, although before you get too excited I should confess that I had Connor bring it over. I don't know a thing about bread."

Sam's eyes lit up. "A Connor creation? Then I know it's going to be good."

"Maybe I should lead with that, tell you the dinner's amazing because Connor was here."

"It does help your pitch."

"So I shouldn't be embarrassed that Connor also seasoned the soup?"

Sam bit her lip, pretending to think. "If the meal is good, you'll still be able to hold your head high."

"Let's hope he didn't intentionally sabotage my whole plan."

"Your plan?" Sam sank into the couch and looked up at him with an eyebrow raised.

Austin took her beer from her hand and placed it next to his on the coffee table. He wrapped an arm around her and then shifted the two of them together so he was lying partway on top of her, leaning her back against the arm of the couch. "My plan to wow you with dinner and then get you into bed."

Sam slithered farther under him. Up against a wall had been fun, but to feel the weight of his body on top of her, the press of his leg between hers—this was what she'd wanted all afternoon. "I don't think that required much of a plan," she said, running her hand through his hair, marveling how it got all spiky and messed up and perfect looking no matter what he did. "You could have served me anything and I'd still wind up in your bed. Or, as it turns out, your couch."

He ran his hands up her stomach, grazing the side of her breast. "Damn," he murmured. "All that work for nothing."

His hand was large, strong. The way he touched her made her feel like he had her completely. Like she belonged.

"I guess now Connor knows who in Gold Mountain is getting some tonight," Sam said with a laugh, tracing her fingers up his back.

"I may have said that I needed dinner tips to impress a lady. I didn't say *which* lady. And I was vague about the terms of the word 'impress.'"

"And how often do you typically call on Connor to save your ass when it comes to entertaining women?"

"Not often enough," Austin conceded.

"And how many unnamed ladies has Connor seen you with recently?"

"Possibly just one."

"Yet again, you go around making me look like the dirty one." She shifted under him, pressing her pelvis up against his thigh.

He pushed back into her just as firmly and rolled up the bottom of her sweater, exposing the skin underneath. "I don't recall you objecting before," he said, his voice low, dropping down to kiss the bare skin. Reminding them both of what they'd done up there on the mountain, desperate for each other against the shelter wall.

She stroked his hair. "Maybe you should turn off the heat under that soup."

Austin agreed that was an excellent idea. He turned off the stove and whistled for Chloe to go to her dog bed upstairs. Suddenly Sam found herself almost...nervous. A quick and dirty whatever-it-was in the stolen minutes in the middle of the day was one thing. The quiet crackle of the fire, smell of warm bread, the home she knew was so important to him—this was something else altogether.

Austin was right. She shouldn't have gotten him the gloves. They were too much, an extravagance her bank account could afford but not her heart. They wouldn't make him think kindly of her when it was over. They'd only serve to remind him of how different, how completely at odds they were.

But when she stood up, she couldn't make herself call this off. He came back to the couch and she wrapped her arms around him, inhaling the scent of him, soap and smoke from the fire, spices from the soup. She felt his solidness against her chest and knew she was like a log on the fire, too much a part of him now to pull back.

It was a good thing she knew how to act without thinking. She had a lifetime of experience pushing aside her nerves and doubt to do whatever she was determined to accomplish. She kissed him and he kissed her back, and that was all she needed to forget her uncertainty. She pushed him back toward the couch and then down so he was sitting. She pulled her sweater over her head as he looked up at her. His hands reached for her and she slapped them away. Austin's eyes flashed.

Sam leaned over him, her breasts cupped in a plum bra accented with lace. She loved the way he looked at her, how his breath quickened when she straddled his lap. She loved the feeling when she ground her hips against him, and the press of his hard-on through his jeans.

When Austin reached his hands up to try and unhook her bra, she grabbed his wrists and threw them back, pinning them against the cushions. He bucked his hips up into her. She pushed back equally hard. This was what she wanted, a chance to let go. There was no worry about right or wrong or slutty or reserved or whatever the ubiquitous chorus of criticisms in her head and all around her came up with next. Right now Sam wasn't nice or a bitch or one of Seattle's most powerful executives. She was just a woman panting in his ear, getting ready to take what was hers.

One hand kept Austin's wrists pinned in place. The other undid the buttons of his shirt. She knew he was strong enough to push her off whenever he wanted, but she also knew the rapid rise and fall of his chest was real. His breath came fast and ragged, his body on edge. He tried to reach for her, but she slammed his arms back into the sofa. "No."

Sam opened his shirt, running her hand over his chest. She ran her lips along the newly exposed skin, licking that incredibly sexy vein that ran across the front of his shoulder and down his biceps. But she had to release his arms to do this, and now he grabbed her hair in his fist and pulled back, making her lift her head. His green eyes were hard and bright in the firelight. He ran a finger down her nose, over her lips. She opened her mouth and sucked on his fingertip.

"Take off my pants," he said hoarsely.

Sam snaked her tongue over his finger and lowered her head, kissing down his stomach, making him squirm. She would do what he demanded, but slowly. In her own way.

She used her teeth to unbutton his jeans. Then she clamped her mouth on the zipper and tugged. Austin let out a groan, thrusting his hips up, desperate to be released. She pulled back the top of his jeans and ran her tongue along the line where his boxer briefs hugged, her mouth watering in anticipation. The sight of that curve where his hips plunged down made her breath catch. She pressed her lips there as she tugged his pants down the rest of the way.

His cock was fully hard in his well-fitted black boxer briefs. She ran her face over it, feeling him through the fabric, a precursor to the way she was going to devour him. Then she hooked her fingers under the band and pulled down just so the tip poked out. She kissed it, wet with suction from her lips, and she thought Austin was going to cry he was so ready for her mouth.

But the more of the fabric she pulled down the more skin she had to kiss, and she teased him, making him wait until he was completely naked and at her command. She might have tortured him even more, but she was desperate, too. She settled with her knees on the ground and slid his length all the way back to her throat.

He was thick and full and she took as much as she could, moving her mouth up and down, sliding her tongue over the tip before plunging back down. She loved how he filled her. She loved how he groaned, a luscious sound, his head thrown back, his eyes closed. His thighs clenched, hips thrusting into her mouth. He ran his fingers through her hair, and when she reached up to press her palm to his stomach, he covered her hand in his, holding it tight. Every so often she caught him lifting his head to look at her, and then the waves of sensation would overcome him and he'd have to drop his head back into the pillows. When she felt his balls tightening in her palm, she wasn't surprised when he pulled her off him.

"Too close." He let out a long, steadying breath. "Way, way too close." He pinched his eyes shut and swore.

Sam lifted her mouth and allowed herself a small, self-satisfied grin. His cock glistened with saliva, beautiful and inviting. She stood up. Austin, panting, limbs gone slack with wanting, gazed up at her.

"You're stunning," he whispered.

She took off her bra and dropped it on his chest. His eyes devoured her breasts, then darted to her pants. She raised an eyebrow, as if in question.

"Dear God," he choked. "Please."

She unzipped her jeans while he watched, mesmerized. She pulled them over her hips, enjoyed the tight slide down her thighs. Stepped out of them as he took her all in. Austin grabbed her ass, drawing her closer. His teeth raked over her panties, his mouth hot on the wet spot she had made.

He was hungry for her. He was tight and hard with wanting. He was going to make her pay for every torturous second she'd withheld her mouth from him.

He ran his hands over her body as though to prove she was here, she was real, she was his. When he pulled her panties down, he slid his finger along her slit, then pressed his chin against her pelvis and looked up, smiling. She ran a hand through his hair that always looked good no matter how messy it was. And then quickly, firmly, she pushed him back so he was lying on the couch again.

Austin might have thought it was his turn, but Sam wasn't done. She climbed on top of him, straddling him, rubbing her sex against the length of his shaft, feeling the tip of his cock against her clit.

"There's a condom in my pocket," he said hoarsely, but Sam shook her head.

"Not yet."

He looked confused until she dragged her legs up his side, straddling his torso, then his chest. He'd seemed to enjoy it so much in the shelter—why shouldn't she make this last as long as she could? She bent down and kissed his lips, soft and warm. Then she slid her knees up by his ears and sat directly on his waiting tongue.

He licked her, devoured her, let her grind her hips into his mouth, his chin. His stubble grated her thighs with a delicious scratch right on the line between pleasure and pain so that she was pulling away even as she thrust down. She felt his arm moving and knew he was stroking himself in the same rhythm that he licked her. The thought of his hand on his cock drove her out of her mind. She pulled away from his mouth—she didn't want this to be over too soon.

"How about that condom now?" she asked and bent over to riffle through his pants. He took the opportunity to come partway up on his elbows, but when she sat over him, ripping the condom wrapper with her teeth, she pushed him back down. His eyes flashed. She slid the condom on.

They held eyes as she lowered herself onto him, feeling

the sweet, sharp sensation of her body unlocking for him.

And then she let him know exactly who he belonged to tonight.

Jim had always accused Sam of wanting to be on top because she had to be in charge, but that wasn't it at all. What Jim didn't understand was that Sam liked being on top because it felt goddamn good—why wasn't that reason enough? And Austin was more than game. He responded to her every move until her whole world narrowed to the sensations mounting within her. His cock filled her; her clit ground right where she wanted it. The twinned pressure built and built until all of a sudden, like a wave, it broke.

She was still drawing out every tremble when Austin picked up his pace. He clung to her hips, positioning her, and came with a cry, lifting his torso to bury his face in the crook of Sam's neck. She rocked her hips with him, savoring every second. When he finished they collapsed together on the couch. She pressed a palm to his chest and felt the gallop of his heart, the way that it raced just for her.

Austin pulled out and took the condom off, but after he threw it away he came back and lay down with her. She settled against his body with a sigh. He was so warm, so comfortable, so hard and soft in all the right ways. Only the grumble of her stomach made them finally pull away.

"I have to feed you if I'm going to keep your energy up," he said as he went to reheat the soup and let the bread warm in the oven.

Sam couldn't stop the grin from spreading across her face. Had he just promised her another round?

As he moved around the kitchen, she peeked over the top of the couch to get a better view of what she was getting to enjoy tonight.

"Damn, that ass," she murmured, staring at him. She hadn't fully realized she'd spoken out loud until he gave a little shake of his butt at the stove. She burst out laughing. She was still giggling when he jumped on the couch and tackled her, kissing and tickling, before finally pulling a blanket over them so they could lie in front of the fire until the soup was done.

Forget what Sam had to deal with tomorrow. *This*, she thought with satisfaction, *is a man who knows how to do a one-night stand.*

Chapter Eleven

Austin pushed back the coffee table so they could sit in front of the fire as they ate. He'd turned off the kitchen lights and was watching the glow of the fire dance on Sam's naked skin. She was flushed and luscious and he wanted to yank off the blankets he'd brought and take her all over again.

"Is this what you always do after a day on the mountain?" Sam ripped a piece of crusty bread from the loaf and dipped it in the soup.

He laughed. "If only I could get Connor to come cook for me every day."

"He certainly helped you out this time."

Austin grinned. "I lure you here with promises of Connor's cooking—"

"Don't forget about the mind-blowing sex." She waved her spoon at him.

He sat up straighter. "Mind-blowing? Really?"

She rolled her eyes.

"As I was saying," he teased, "I lure you here and get you all comfortable, so by the time you realize it's mostly leftovers or whatever's happening at Mack's, it's too late."

"Too late for what?" Sam asked, and Austin flushed. He'd better watch himself before his mouth ran away with him. It was easy to say these things. It was much, much harder to follow through.

"Just too late." He took a sip of beer. "That's all."

He thought he saw her give a half smile, but her hair fell over her shoulder and shielded her face. He reached over and brushed the strands back. He was right, she was smiling. It made something well up inside him. "I have to tell you something," he said.

Sam looked at him in immediate concern. "It's not a big deal," he said quickly, wondering what she thought he was about to spill. "I just wanted you to know I've never taken anyone there before."

"Where?"

"The shelter. On the mountain. I don't just mean for, you know." He waggled his eyebrows. "I mean I've never shown it to anyone, period."

Sam lowered her spoon. "Never?"

"I'm sure other people know about it—I've seen tracks. But I've never brought someone there. I've never been there with anyone else."

Sam looked at the fire. He wondered what she was thinking. Maybe it was stupid and didn't mean a thing. Maybe it meant everything and would scare her away. But right when he was about to tell her to forget it, it was just a thought that had popped into his head, because he hadn't wanted her to think he was taking all sorts of women to his special sex spot or whatever—he could say this with a laugh, he was already practicing his indifference in his head—she set her bowl out of the way and scooted closer to him. She rested her head on his shoulder, her hair cascading down his arm, and he knew she understood.

"You were supposed to show me your knee," she said after a long pause in which they watched the flames leap in a mesmerizing show.

Austin laughed, a nervous tightening inside. Just because he'd told her one thing didn't mean he wanted to get into *everything*. "I was just kidding about that."

"It's the whole reason I came over. Your ass is so-so. I really wanted you naked so I could see that sexy patella of yours."

"You know, you're kind of an asshole," Austin said. "I'll have you know some women have appreciated this very fine behind."

Sam burst out laughing. "Oh, honey." She stroked his arm. "I've been called *so* much worse."

Austin wanted to know what that was supposed to mean, but she was already going after him so she could flip off the blanket and get to his knee. He let her pin him down, commenting how much he liked the view as her breasts hung close. She pressed her palm over his mouth to silence him, then replaced her hand with her lips and kissed him.

"The knee," she murmured, sliding her naked body along his. "Tell me the story about your knee."

He hesitated. The need to *tell someone* ached constantly inside him, just like the pain in his knee. If only he could get it out, unlock the secret from that place it was buried, maybe all his old hurts would finally heal. He pictured himself saying the words, telling the story, as though that was all it would take to make him okay.

But he couldn't do it. As he shifted to show Sam where the pins and wire bored in to keep his leg together, he heard a thud that might have been Chloe upstairs or might have been in his mind. His mother's suitcase dropping as his father lunged. Glint of metal. Somebody's cry.

His heart raced, sweat on his brow. It was too much, he couldn't say it, he couldn't let her know how weak he was, how unlike the person she thought she knew.

Sam was looking down and didn't notice what was happening to him. She traced the mess of scars with her fingertips. "Ouch," she whispered, and pressed her lips to his knee.

"Sometimes it's stiff," Austin said, trying to keep his voice steady. "But you get used to the pain."

She drew herself up so she was nestled against his shoulder, the blankets pulled around them as the fire sputtered and danced.

"The accident really happened two weeks before the Olympics? You couldn't have had worse timing."

Austin imagined jumping up, grabbing her clothes, sending her into the night. Hitting the gym until he couldn't breathe from exhaustion instead of from the fear tightening his throat. He wanted to forget, not bring it up all over again.

There was no way he could tell her the truth.

He found, though, that he couldn't follow through with his usual lies.

"I used to spend every second wishing things had turned out differently. But you know what?" He shifted so he was facing her, their legs intertwined. "I can't say what might have happened instead. I might not have medaled. I might have been injured later, in some other way. I could have had an amazing career. I could have been disappointed." He shrugged. "I guess there's simply no way to know."

"You sound at peace," Sam said softly. She ran a finger along the side of his face. Austin pretended to snap his jaw to catch her finger in his teeth. She pulled back just in time, then reached for him again. Her eyes were soft. He wondered what she was thinking, if she believed him. It sounded so good, he almost believed himself.

"When you do something where you could be injured, you always know everything you've worked for could be over in a heartbeat. Sometimes I feel like I made my peace before I was even hurt. I knew it was coming. I knew what I was going to do."

The truth surprised him. He was talking about skiing, but he was also, unbeknownst to Sam, telling her about his father. In some way, he'd known exactly what was going to happen when his father reached for that hammer. And he'd let it happen anyway.

"Other times I feel like you're never prepared. Even when you choose, even when you think you know, you can't predict what's going to happen. You can't say where your life is going to go."

You can't understand, when you're yelling at your father to hit you, exactly how long twelve months of rehab is going to feel.

Sam leaned back, resting her back against the couch. "I guess I'm still at that crossroad, trying to think everything through. I think I know what I'm doing and then…"

"And then what?" Austin asked when she didn't go on.

"And then, surprise, I have no idea what's next."

"Well, yeah. That sounds about right." Austin shifted and started stacking their dishes, ready to move the conversation onto less personal ground. He knew this was a chance for them to open up more to each other, but he'd said all he could. He didn't want to push Sam to share what she was referring to and then have her turn around and ask the same questions about him. Questions he never answered, for anybody, no matter how beautiful they were. Especially when they were only around for such a short time.

"Dessert?" he proposed.

"You think of everything." Sam began to scramble up.

"Stay there," Austin said. "I'll bring it to you. I hope you like chocolate."

"Naked chocolate eating? Have I died? Is this heaven?

Are you real?"

Austin laughed. "Do you mind if I let Chloe down? She's used to being the only girl I have in front of the fireplace."

"Not at all! I didn't mean to make her jealous."

"She's a little spoiled, I'll admit. Just wait here and I'll be back in a sec."

He was happy to see her draw the blankets around her and get comfortable on the couch, apparently undisturbed by his revelations—or lack thereof. He could feel his heart rate settling back to normal, the sudden sweat that had broken out beginning to cool. He hadn't said too much. He didn't have to be afraid.

They spent the rest of the evening in front of the fire, the remnants of cake and coffee on the table. Chloe lay on her bed while Sam and Austin curled up together on the couch. He didn't know when he fell asleep, only that when he woke up the fire had died down to embers and Sam was asleep, too. He tried to get up without waking her, but she stirred.

"Hey," he whispered, brushing her hair off her cheek. "It's late."

"Mmm," she murmured.

"I can drive you back if you want."

Her eyes opened sleepily. "Hmm?"

"I said I can drive you to your car." He paused. "Or you can spend the night here."

"Driving back means cold and cold means clothes and clothes are terrible." She tugged the blanket tighter around her.

"I like the way you think."

"Will you think I'm too presumptuous if I admit I brought a toothbrush with me?"

"Now I *really* like the way you think. But let's go upstairs, it'll be warmer. There are blankets on the bed and you can borrow pajamas if you're cold. Unless of course you brought your own?"

Sam grinned sheepishly. "Part of my presumptuousness meant I wasn't exactly thinking about clothes."

Austin fed Chloe and steered Sam upstairs, the blanket trailing behind her as she walked with it wrapped around herself. He liked this funny, sleepy side of her, a little out of it, too tired to be clever or on guard. For a moment something clenched in his chest at the sight of the light through the crack underneath the bathroom door—this was his space, no one was supposed to be here. But when she came out, still naked, hair messy, eyes heavy with sleep, he couldn't help but reach for her again. They fell asleep wrapped tightly together in the middle of the bed, even though there was plenty of room.

Chapter Twelve

Sam woke up alone.

"Austin?" she murmured, but nobody answered. She looked around the bedroom, the bathroom, peered over the edge of the overhang down into the living room below. She didn't hear him in the kitchen. She didn't know where he was.

She opened his closet, scolding herself as she did so. She shouldn't go through his things. But her clothes were downstairs in a tangle on the floor. The reminder sent heat coursing through her, mixed with a heavy dose of—no, not regret, she checked herself. Sadness.

Sadness that it all had to end.

She pulled on a button-down shirt of his that went to her thighs and found a pair of thick socks. She knew she looked ridiculous, but she liked the idea of making him laugh.

Wherever he was.

At least this wasn't the equivalent of waking up in her hotel room and finding him gone. He wouldn't peace out on her in his own place, right?

She used her fingers to make her hair semipresentable

and padded downstairs. There was coffee in a pot, and she poured herself a mug. No Chloe, no Austin. She found her phone in her jeans pocket and picked up just enough signal to log in to her email. She sat at the kitchen table and tried to tackle the onslaught of work that had rolled in since she'd been gone. She had to admit the whole thing seemed to be running fine without her. But there were emails to respond to, deals to keep on top of, new clients to woo. Major clients didn't like feeling they were paying an arm and a leg to be bounced around among subordinates. This was what Kane Enterprises was selling—the personalized touch.

Not the *very* personal touch she'd given Mr. Reede, but she'd come to Gold Mountain to give him the attention needed to see this sale go through. She'd had her night, and now it was time to face what she had to accomplish today.

Before she could think through how that was going to work, the front door opened and a very snowy German shepherd bounded through.

"Good girl, Chloe," Austin cooed. "You tell those squirrels who's boss." Then he caught sight of Sam at the table. "Sorry." He winced as Chloe shook the snow out of her fur right where Sam was sitting. "We try to do that outside, but it doesn't always work."

Sam laughed, shielding her phone. Chloe promptly stuck her nose in Sam's lap, no doubt attracted to the scent of Austin's shirt. Sam ruffled the scruff of her neck. "Did you have a good walk?" she asked the dog. "Did you terrorize the mean little squirrels?"

"Have you been up long?" Austin asked as he hung up his jacket and took off his boots.

"Maybe twenty minutes. I got some coffee."

"I meant to leave a note that we were out. I guess I'm not so used to having company."

The admission startled Sam. No girlfriends? Not even

one-night stands?

She pushed the thought from her mind. She didn't want to think about Austin with other women. She didn't want to think of herself as a one-night thing.

When Austin rattled off options for breakfast, Sam knew she couldn't transform into work mode just yet. "I make a mean French toast," he said. "No Connor necessary."

"I definitely think you should show off for me," she said.

"Shit, now the pressure's on."

She stood and hooked her finger through his belt loop, pulling him toward her. Snow still clung to his lashes. She pictured him rolling around with the dog, racing her through the woods behind his house. The woods they wouldn't be able to run in once Sam had her way, because they wouldn't be his anymore.

She squeezed her eyes shut. *Don't think that, don't think that.* "I'm not wearing any panties under this shirt of yours," she whispered. "If you make a girl a good breakfast, wonder what you'll get in return?"

She meant to pull away—it was just a tease, she was only trying to play—but Austin had her pushed against the wall so quickly it took her breath away. He kissed her hard, his hands sliding up the bottom of the shirt, over her hips and her ass, along the inside of her thighs. He pressed his thumb to her clit, just hard enough to make her throb. Not hard enough to stop her from trying to press down.

"And what is it you want?" he panted in her ear. He flicked his other thumb over her nipples, hard and straining through her shirt. "Hmm?"

"Guess I should know not to tease a man in the morning," Sam murmured, straining to get closer to him and relieve the ache he was making build between her thighs.

"You're lucky I let you sleep in."

Sam pictured him climbing on top of her, his cock

throbbing, not waiting to take what he wanted from her. She knew he could feel her dampness in his hand. "You should have woken me up."

"Next time I just might." He brushed her clit. Her thighs clenched in response. That "next time" seemed to ring out between them.

"I was promised French toast," she said with a squirm.

He pulled away so suddenly her whole body ached. "I know. I'd better feed you before I fuck you."

Sam tilted her head back so it hit the wall and let out a sigh she felt all the way to her toes. Oh, God. She was in trouble.

"That's what I thought last night," she said, "but that wasn't the order I wound up wanting."

"Tough luck." He kissed her nose. "I'm starving."

He really did make good French toast, sprinkled with cinnamon and maple syrup from just over the border in Canada. She cut up strawberries and made more coffee and they sat at the table, Sam's leg curling up the inside of Austin's thigh.

"Where'd the recipe come from?" she asked. "I'm picturing childhood brunches, parents being all cute together… Do you have siblings?" She licked maple syrup off her fork. She knew she was being reckless, making things too personal, but the fact that this was ending today made it impossible not to soak up what she could.

She was surprised when Austin's face darkened. But then the cloud was gone, so quickly she wondered if she'd made up the shadow she thought she'd seen. "Not so much from my parents as one of the things I picked up along the way."

"So, an ex-girlfriend," Sam concluded.

"Whatever, she was always too stingy with the cinnamon." Austin rolled his eyes and slid a hand up Sam's bare thigh.

"At least you got something good out of it."

He shrugged. Her phone vibrated on the table. She never should have turned it on to check her messages. The momentary respite had been too good to last.

"Work?" Austin raised an eyebrow.

"Sorry," she grumbled.

"Better than a boyfriend."

Sam stared at him. "You think I'm cheating on someone with you?"

"No, but you haven't really told me much about yourself. I don't even know what you do."

"I told you—sales." Her palm felt slippery as she reached for the phone.

"Twenty-four seven? With a scary-sounding board?"

She shrugged. "That's the job." She glanced briefly at the text—Steven wanting to know when the meeting for today was set. At least he hadn't typed the words "Mr. Reede," but she put her phone facedown on the table anyway. "It's not life or death, though. There's nothing I have to deal with now."

Couldn't Steven wait? She wasn't going to corner Austin while she was wearing nothing but his button-down shirt.

"What about you?" she asked, changing the subject. "What do you have to do today?"

"I'm not on ski patrol this morning."

He said it casually, but Sam narrowed her eyes. "Is that usually the case? Or just a nice little coincidence?" She plucked a strawberry slice off his plate and popped it into her mouth.

"No need to concern yourself with the inner machinations of Gold Mountain staff."

She laughed. "You were awfully cocky, thinking I was going to stay over."

"You're the one who brought your toothbrush." He swatted

her hand away from his plate where she was cleaning up the last of his breakfast. "I feel bad, though. You're paying through the nose for that hotel room and you didn't even use it."

Sam shrugged. "Doesn't matter. It's just one night, and anyway"—she winked—"I'd say last night was better than sitting in bed by myself with pay-per-view."

"Why watch it when you can live it." His hand, her thigh. She spread her legs in the chair.

His lips tasted like syrup, and she teased him with her tongue. Her phone vibrated, and this time it didn't stop. Goddammit, Steven had an uncanny sense of timing. Clearly since she hadn't responded to his text within five and a half seconds, he'd decided to call.

"Do you have to get that?" Austin asked.

Sam wished she knew the answer to his question. Things must have been getting heated at the office if Steven was so intent on confirming the signing with Mr. Reede was going through. But how could she reassure him she was on top of it while Austin was sitting right there, talking about what they were doing that day?

"You don't already have a lift ticket, do you?" he asked.

Sam shook her head.

"Okay, good. I don't want you to waste it."

A lift ticket? That was nothing. He had no idea how much she risked losing for him. Her phone vibrated again. God, Steven was pissed. Or worried. Or both. Mentally she told him to cool it and pressed ignore. "Even if I already did, Austin, you should know by now I'd blow it off for you."

He shook his head. "Those tickets are so expensive, I'd never ask you to do that."

She felt so guilty, her stomach ached. She couldn't have said how much a ski patroller and racing coach made, but it clearly wasn't enough to buy new gloves. Austin could have no clue that buying a lift ticket she didn't use wouldn't make a single difference in the life of Samantha Kane.

He told her he'd lend her some ski pants, and she was telling him okay, thinking it wouldn't be so bad to spend the morning together before he took her to her car and she finally came clean, when the phone vibrated again.

"Sales?" His eyebrow rose.

Her heart raced, torn between a fear of getting caught and a fear of what might happen if she actually blew Steven off and didn't pick up.

But she simply shrugged and said, "Things are busy," and Austin seemed to buy it.

"It's funny," he said as he stacked the dishes. "I was the one expecting all these calls today. I thought Kane Enterprises wouldn't stop bugging me about setting up this meeting, but I haven't heard a thing. Meanwhile you're on vacation, sort of, and your office won't leave you alone." He wiped his hands on a towel. "Maybe we should trade."

Sam snorted. Fuck if she knew what to say to that. "I'd make a terrible ski coach," she declared.

"That's not true, Amelia loved you."

"Amelia loved not having to ski with a bloody nose."

"Hey, that kid's tough—don't underestimate her. If that were a race day, she'd never have quit."

"I never said she was a quitter," Sam said. "But you do remember she's in high school, right?"

"Age has nothing to do with it. Amelia's got a shot to go far, and she's going to."

"And if something happens to her? You yourself said skiers know they could be injured any time." Sam remembered what Amelia had said in the bathroom, how she didn't have time for a boyfriend when all she did was ski. "What if she decides she wants to do something else with her life? What if this isn't her plan?"

The look on Austin's face made her realize she'd gone too

far.

"I don't want Amelia to shy away from what she can accomplish," he said, his voice low, level, so serious it was almost cold. "It's important she learns not to back down."

Sam wanted to know if they were still talking about Amelia. But the subtext was clear: *back off.* Austin went to get the ski pants. The conversation was over.

Once upon a time, Sam had a plan for how her life and her career were going to progress. Then her father died, and everything changed. It didn't matter that she hadn't been ready, that she'd thought there'd be more time before the inevitable came to pass. Her father didn't wait until things were convenient for her to make her CEO. He died during surgery—a risk, of course, but they were in the risk business. No matter how much they'd calculated the odds, she'd never really expected it would be like that, so final, his heart beating and then not.

Obviously Austin knew there was no such thing as plans. He'd had to remake his life, too. Only instead of realizing nothing was set, he'd gone in the opposite direction. Here was his star skier, and she was going to win. Here were his gloves, and he wasn't going to replace them. Here was his property, and not a single tree could change.

Sam knew those things weren't comparable, and yet watching Austin's back as he left the kitchen, it sure felt like that. And she was the one who wanted to change his home, his town—hell, even his gloves. She was the one asking whether Amelia's plans might someday change, asking whether Austin had too much wrapped up in a kid he'd convinced himself was going to make his own failed Olympic dreams come true.

It wasn't a fight, exactly. But it wasn't the note she wanted them to end on. It certainly wasn't the way to segue into the sale. When Steven called again, she texted him *Later* and silenced her phone.

Chapter Thirteen

Austin went outside to warm up the truck and brush off the dusting of snow that had fallen in the night. Yesterday's clouds were lifting, exposing stretches of blue trying to make their way through. It was going to be a beautiful day.

If he didn't blow it first.

What was his deal, getting so defensive about Amelia? He'd thought he was finally figuring out this whole intimacy thing, like taking Sam to the shelter, even inviting her to wake up in his bed. And then the next thing he knew he was closing conversations, turning his back on Sam when he went to get the ski pants, barely giving her a glance or a word as she put everything on.

"Don't do this," he muttered to himself as he went in to tell her the truck was ready. "Don't ruin something that might actually work."

Not that he knew where anything with Sam was going. Didn't she have a busy job? A life in Seattle? Whatever it was, it kept her flush with cash, judging by the gloves she'd bought him. The thought made him burn up inside. He couldn't say yes to them. But how had he actually brought himself to say no?

He didn't even know why he'd gotten so touchy about Amelia. *I'm not pushing her away*, he told himself sternly. *I'm protecting my life.* So what if he didn't want to tell her everything that had happened with his knee, or listen to her criticize his coaching? If she stuck around, he'd open up more.

If that wasn't going to happen, so be it. He hoped this wouldn't be their last day together. But he didn't want to be crushed if she was going to announce that it had been fun, but it was time for her to go home.

Sam seemed to have come to a similar conclusion, because when she hopped in the truck she was cheerful as usual, as though he hadn't been terse. Because she didn't care? Because she was already planning her escape? He didn't even know how to ask, because they weren't enough of a thing for him to find out what they were or were not.

But she was wonderful right now. And right now, that was enough.

"Where are we going?" Sam asked. "Or is this another one of your Austin surprises?"

"It's not far," he said cryptically.

"It's not skiing, because we don't have any gear. But it can't be driving or you wouldn't have me wearing this sexy getup." She gestured to his ski pants, which managed to fit her after she rolled the bottoms.

"Does that narrow it down?" Austin asked.

"Nope."

Sam pulled out her phone and checked something, then put it away. Austin was about to comment—did she ever go without that thing?—but he bit it back. That was what Austin usually did. Once he saw the crack, he picked at it and picked at it until it widened and the whole foundation fell down. He didn't want to do that this time, not when he didn't even know how long he'd have Sam anyway.

"I told work I'm unavailable for a few hours," Sam offered without his prompting.

"It's okay." He looked at the road.

"It's not, I know. But this is how it is with me, and I'm lucky I can be here instead of in the office."

The subtext being *Drop me off at the corner if you have a problem with it.*

Austin reached over and squeezed her knee as he drove. "Really," he said, and this time he meant it. "I don't know why I'm so testy this morning."

"Too much to have someone spend the night?" Sam asked, and Austin wondered what it was about her, how she could push through every angle and sink her teeth right into the sore spot inside.

He withdrew his hand and kept his eyes on the road. "It's not a thing that happens very often," he finally said.

This time she was the one who reached over and touched his leg. "I can go."

"No." He looked at her. "Seriously. No."

"Good." Sam sat back, satisfied. By the time Austin parked the truck, they were holding hands across the front seat. It shouldn't have put Austin at ease. But it did.

"Where are we?" Sam asked.

"Sue and Jesse own Mack Daddy's—you know, the Dipper."

Sam looked out the window. "Uh-huh."

"Jesse's got something I want to borrow."

Sam pointed to the snowmobile sitting out in the driveway, by Jesse's truck. "You don't mean—"

Austin grinned. "What do you say?"

Sam opened the door and hopped out. "Coming?" she called to him. He turned off the ignition and pocketed the key, laughing at her. He should have known better than to think she wouldn't want to go.

They walked up the front steps of the house and knocked on the door. Jesse and Sue were in their sixties and had been living in Gold Mountain for the last thirty years. They'd been among the first to welcome Austin when he moved in, and he borrowed Jesse's snowmobile more than a few times every year.

"Of course," Jesse said when Austin introduced Sam and asked if he could take it for a spin. "You going to Pine Points?"

"You guessed it." Austin grinned then turned to Sam. "You need a snowmobile to get to a lot of the mountain passes when everything's snowed in. I only go out when the snow's deep enough to protect the topsoil, though, and Jesse's got a good silencer so the engine won't disturb the wildlife."

"Not many roads around here," Jesse added. "But that's all about to change." He sighed.

They were sitting in the kitchen, drinking a fresh pot of coffee Jesse had put on. Austin wasn't sure he needed any more caffeine, but he wouldn't say no to Jesse's offer. Sue was down in Bellingham grocery shopping, and Austin knew the man was lonely, semiretired and not sure what to do when it was too snowy to tinker in the yard.

"What's about to change?" Sam asked, stirring her coffee with a spoon.

"You must have heard how Kane Enterprises is coming in here."

"Sure," Sam said. She blew on the coffee and glanced at Austin as she took a sip.

"Sam's probably heard more about the Kanes than she ever wanted to."

Jesse chuckled. "They still after you?"

"I know you had reasons to sell, and I'm okay with that," Austin said. "But you know me." He shrugged. "I just can't."

"I hear you. It's such a shame when you think of how

much this whole place is going to be paved."

"Surely it's not going to be the *whole* place," Sam said.

"A damn lot of it. They're buying the plot from here up to the mountain, then down to the Points"—he gestured vaguely south—"and over to the Cascade Loop." He took a noisy sip. "And that's only part of it."

Once Jesse got going, he could talk forever. Austin hoped Sam wouldn't mind, but she was leaning forward, rapt, asking him more questions about what was going to happen to the land.

"Now me and Sue, we got the promise of a fat check from the Kanes if this deal goes through. We're supposed to hear as soon as something's signed with the management up at Gold, and the Hendersons—" He leaned over toward Sam to explain, "That's one of the families who own a lot of the land up here. There are a few who are in on the sale." Sam nodded, following along. "Well, once that goes through we'll sell the Dipper. Everything's going to go."

"But why are you selling if you don't want to?" Sam asked.

"What am I going to do? The Kanes can outlast me. They can build around me. They can do anything to push me out. And the size of that check." He whistled. "I know it's nothing to them, but how can I say no to that? Austin here can tell them where to put their millions, but I've got a boy just out of college, a daughter at UW studying to be a nurse. They've got bills, loans. How am I supposed to say no when this can help my kids?"

"Then maybe it's not such a bad thing that the Kanes are coming in," Sam suggested.

But Jesse shook his head, as Austin knew he would. "Just because I'm taking their money doesn't mean I support what they do. Just because I know it'll help my kids doesn't mean I don't wish there were some other way." He raised his chin toward Austin. "I admire this guy. He's got principles, and he sticks with them. I only wish it made a difference in the long run."

He sighed into his empty mug. Austin could feel the weight that lay over Jesse, the same weight that had settled over all of them since they learned the talk they'd heard about for years was actually going through.

"Sam's just up for a few days, and I wanted to show her some of the land. Take her out before so much of it changes," Austin said.

Jesse brightened. "It looks like the clouds are lifting and it'll be nothing but blue by the time you get out. You got everything you need? You have warm gloves, honey? It gets cold in the wind."

Sam assured him she was fully outfitted. They thanked him for the coffee and set out.

Austin had always thought he had everything he needed—a team to coach, tracks to ski, good friends, and a loyal dog for company. He didn't need his life to change. And yet something felt different when he was with Sam. As they settled onto Jesse's snowmobile, her arms around his chest felt so right, he wondered how he'd managed to take this ride so many times without realizing how alone he had been.

"You ever ridden one of these?" he asked.

Sam shook her head against his back. "It feels like being on a Jet Ski, though."

"You've been jet skiing?"

"In the San Juans."

Of course. Her family probably took all sorts of summer vacations together, too.

"A little warmer than this," he said.

Sam laughed. "Anything is warmer than this." She burrowed closer to his back.

"Don't forget to hold on," Austin said, even though it wasn't like she needed the reminder. He felt her thighs clench around him.

"I'm not letting go," she whispered in his ear, and Austin was right back in the kitchen that morning, his fingers sliding up her thighs. Why had he wanted to do something that involved bundling up in so many layers when they could have been back home taking all those layers off?

But as soon as he pulled the throttle and eased them toward the trail, he knew. If Sam wanted to get a sense of why he loved this land, why everyone who lived here did, this was what she had to see. He didn't know what her life was like in Seattle, what meetings and appointments and corporate whatever took up her time. But she was here now, and this was what home meant to him.

The trail headed back toward the woods then climbed steadily to one of the ridges that linked up to the peak of Gold Mountain and extended to the spine of mountains beyond. He shifted his weight forward as the slope pitched, and she responded with him, so that even out here, fully clothed, separated by all the layers between them, it still felt like they moved as one, shoulder to shoulder, hip to hip, her legs firm around his. As the slope evened out, he reached a hand behind and rubbed along the inside of her thigh, feeling her breath quicken in his ear.

And then they were climbing again, up steady switchbacks along the eastern face of the mountain that rose as though a mirror to Gold Mountain, the two peaks facing each other across the valley between.

Austin pulled back on the throttle and asked Sam, "How high do you want to go?"

Her response didn't surprise him. "How high can we go?"

"We can go all the way," he said, and she squeezed his waist. He revved the engine and plowed up, so fast she had to cling tight to him.

He brought the snowmobile to a stop above the tree line

but below the final crest of the peak, where it grew too steep to safely take it the rest of the way. This was why he'd outfitted them with chains on the bottom of their boots, metal loops that made an X over the sole and kept them from sliding back.

Sam climbed off the snowmobile, her scarf wrapped tight around her neck, Austin's spare pair of goggles oversize on her face. She stood uncertainly, as though she didn't trust the chains to hold her.

"Let's go," he said, before she had time to get too cold standing around and psych herself out.

"Where?"

He pointed up. Sam looked at him as though he were crazy. "You want to climb the rest of the way?"

"It's not far," he promised.

Sam squinted up, evaluating. "I'm not sure what that means in Austin skispeak," she said.

"It means you climb until you think you can't make it, and right when your legs are about to give out—ta-da! You're there."

"Great," she said. "It's not like I spent yesterday on a mogul run, so my legs aren't sore at all."

"You're sore?" he asked.

"I haven't skied in years, and in case you forgot, I was the one doing the work last night." She reached for his hips, and he had a flash of her body arched over him, her thighs wrapped around his face. His cock stirred at the hope it wasn't only a memory of the past but a promise of more to come. He wanted her right there, buried in the snow. But as incredible as the view was from here, it was only going to get better. And that was what he wanted Sam to see.

Austin pulled on the low braid hanging out from under Sam's hat and brought his lips close to her ear. "I haven't forgotten a thing." He swung the braid over her shoulder. "You might want to unzip your jacket a little. Things are about to heat up."

Austin had a route he liked, a short but sweet ascent to a 360-degree view untouched by crowds or ski lifts.

He heard Sam breathing steadily beside him, but she didn't once flag. He had a feeling she wouldn't slow down no matter what. When they stopped to rest, Austin promised Sam he knew a great massage therapist in town.

"Her name's Claire, she works on my leg once a week. I'll call when we get back. You definitely shouldn't leave before making an appointment."

Sam seemed excited by the prospect, but immediately Austin wished he could take it back. He didn't want to talk about Sam leaving, not while the snow sparkled in the sun and the diamond white of the valley spread farther below them with each step they climbed.

Not that the first part of what he'd said was any better, letting her know his weaknesses, drawing attention back to his leg. He was getting sloppy, careless. Letting her in just so he'd feel justified later in pushing her out. He hated it when she asked, "You get a massage every week?"

But when he told her it helped loosen him up after all the skiing he did, she seemed to accept the answer without question, and he didn't know whether that was better or worse than someone who demanded to know every little detail about why, how, how long. It had taken him forever to tell Claire how he was really injured, even when, every week, she reminded him she couldn't properly treat him if she didn't know the problem. He'd sort of hated her for asking even though she was just doing her job.

They climbed until there was nothing but snow-covered rock, just them and the snow and the sky. Austin's legs burned, but it was the kind of pain that didn't actually hurt. He grabbed her hand for the last few steps. "Look up," he said.

She gasped.

With no trees to get in the way, the wind was strong, sending plumes of snow into the air. But they were so warm from the climb it felt good, the cold on their faces balancing the heat radiating from their pumping hearts. Austin pointed over the vast expanse of the Cascades, white peaks pointing up to the sky.

"Some days you can see to Canada, to the mountains farther north." He shifted his finger west. "And the Olympics, on the other side of Seattle. Mount Rainier is down that way. And then all of this." He stretched in a wide 360, taking in the expansive view. "All of this is why I'm here." He looked down at her. "This is why, no matter what the Kanes do, I want to keep my part of the woods untouched. I can't control the entire Cascades." He laughed. "But I can control that."

"It's beautiful," Sam said. "It's breathtaking. I can't even say what it is. There aren't any words."

"They say what's his name, the guy who started the whole thing, the one who used to own the company—"

"Bill Kane," Sam said.

"They say he traveled all over these parts and drafted the blueprints himself, deciding where to build. He didn't want to just hire out some contractors. He had this whole vision, or whatever you want to call it, of what he was going to do."

Sam didn't answer. He went on.

"But I don't understand how that's possible. I don't understand how anyone could come here and look at this view and think, *Hey, here's a great place to build.*"

"You really love it here," Sam said quietly.

A soft noise escaped from the back of Austin's throat. "Maybe the problem is me."

"Maybe it's not a problem," Sam said. "Maybe it won't turn out like you think."

"I know Gold Mountain needs help. I know it needs money, and new equipment, and that if it wants to compete with the other resorts and keep its doors open, it has to expand. But everything I've read about the proposal is focused on new roads, new hotels, amenities for people who don't even live here."

He looked over at Sam. "I'm sorry, I'm yammering."

She shook her head. "No. It's enough up here to make you think."

"I'm glad you like it."

She lifted the goggles, so he could see the dark flash of her eyes, the way she seemed to look not just at him but through him, into some deep place he thought he'd long ago closed the door on.

"I get that you don't share these things with just anyone. I want you to know that I know that, and it means something to me."

He didn't have a response, so he pulled her close to him, his arms tight around her, both of them looking over the great, open world splayed down below. He could look at this view for hours, forever, and never get tired of it. The mountains changed in every season, with every snowfall. He liked the shelter on Gold Mountain, where he felt safe, on solid ground. But he craved the expanse of the peaks, feeling the pull in his chest as though he were about to dive into nothing. The trees and sky and rock called to him the way the racecourse once called to him, taunting him with possibility. Teasing him with promises of flight.

"I can see how important this place is to you," Sam went on, linking her arm through his. He watched the breath come from her mouth, the beauty of her warmth in the middle of the cold. "But things change. Everything changes. The things we love—they never stay the same. And even if we think we know what happens next, we think we've got it all figured out, it never works out like we'd planned."

"It's not that I don't want this place to change," he argued.

"It's how it changes. It's what it changes for. There's so much need here. Kane Enterprises is right—there aren't enough jobs. You heard Jesse—his kids are in Seattle, Bellingham. We lose talent to Portland, Vancouver, all over the place. The whole point is that Amelia has the talent to *leave*. That's what people aspire to. Going away.

"We need jobs, and opportunities, and things to keep people here. But I don't think that has to take the form of a giant resort that caters to rich outsiders. The whole point is that this place is stunning, accessible, has tons to do year-round, yet it isn't super built-up or a giant traffic jam. I'm sure Kane Enterprises has done its research, and the proposal's been approved or however that works. Obviously the other parties have been willing to sell, and the community is going along with it. But that doesn't make it *right*, Sam. That doesn't mean the people here have really had a choice."

"But don't you think Kane Enterprises is thinking about sustainability and has plans for roads that won't lock everything up?"

Austin shook his head. "They're not thinking about this from the perspective of people who live and travel here. They're seeing the map from the top down instead of from the inside."

Sam squirmed around in his arms. He wondered if he'd said something wrong. "How do you know that? Why would you think the worst-case scenario is the one that's gong to come true?"

Austin couldn't help laughing a little at that. "Experience. But I've followed what Kane has done elsewhere—in downtown Seattle, in that development along Puget Sound, in the San Juans. Did you hear about that uproar on Bainbridge, when they knocked down the ferry building and built that whole monstrosity?"

"That makes it so much easier to get to and from the

island," Sam pointed out.

"That puts twice as many people on the ferry so the company makes twice as much, as do the Kane-owned parking garages, and the vendors who now have to buy permits from Kane. And then when they get to the island, there's no place to put all those people. It's like an amusement park ride." He turned toward her, agitation making his heart beat like a drum. "There's the land that's going to be destroyed so some people can have a second or third luxury home or whatever, but there are additional costs, too. My friend Abbi is a naturalist, she has tons of information about wildlife disruption. And I spent my undergrad studying this area, environmental management, that sort of thing. I know I sound dopey, but it's just—does Kane have anything in its plans to reduce waste, make the lodges low impact, cover additional snowmaking needs? Anything? Because nothing we've seen of the proposal deals with any of that and I'm…"

He looked down at his hands, embarrassed by his outburst. The duct tape around his fingers was peeling. He'd have to apply another layer—preferably not when Sam was around.

Sam cocked her head and looked at him intently. "Say you had unlimited funds. Money is no object. You can do whatever you damn well please. Say you're head of Kane Enterprises and have all their resources at your disposal. What would you do here?"

"Oh, man." He laughed. "I think we'd freeze to death before I got through that whole list."

"You actually have ideas?"

He was hurt that she sounded surprised.

"I just told you I studied this."

"I thought you, uh, skied."

He raised an eyebrow. "I can do other things, too, you know. After my ski career tanked, I was still young. Clearly I had to do *something*. I came to Washington for school and got my degree in environmental management. I only lasted a year in an office, but hey. At least I tried." He turned to look at her. "It's not like I haven't thought about this. I live here. My whole livelihood depends on the mountain. So I definitely have ideas about where to put the new runs, set up facilities on the mountains, what the condos can be like. I just think it can be done without, you know, completely destroying so many people's property."

Sam nodded, but something about how closely she was paying attention, as though his thoughts actually mattered, made him feel ridiculous for talking like this at all.

"But it's not like anyone would listen to me," he said with a sigh. "What with the whole fact that I don't have unlimited funds and am very much not a Kane. The only reason they want to talk to me is to strong-arm me into selling. Or something—I don't know. It's weird they still haven't called."

He picked up a clump of fluffy snow and fashioned it into a ball, but when he threw it, the whole thing fell away like a dandelion puff, the snow drifting before the ball hit the ground.

Sam kissed his cheek. "I'm listening."

Then she took a ball of snow and shoved it in his face.

The surprise of cold and wet made him shout and he was on her in an instant, pinning her down, the two of them throwing snow at each other like they were kids having a brawl on a snow day. They laughed until they were shrieking from the snow dripping under their jackets and scarves. But as they raced back down the trail they grew warm again, panting, flushed, and breathless as they climbed back on the snowmobile.

"I bet the Cascade has a nice hot tub," Austin mused, starting the engine.

Sam sat behind him and traced a lazy finger over his back. "I was just thinking about that fireplace of yours. A little more private?" She reached around with her other hand and squeezed the inside of his thigh. When he groaned, she went farther. All that fabric between her hand and his cock and still she was making him hard. It was the way she touched him, panting in his ear, grinding her body against his back.

"You can't do this to me," he groaned.

"Can't?" Sam flicked the flesh of his earlobe that stuck out under his hat. "That sounds like a challenge."

"Oh, no, you don't." Austin turned the engine off. Fast. Even Sam paused in her ministrations, not sure what he was about to do.

Good. She couldn't always be in charge all the time. Not that he minded the way she'd thrown him on the sofa and done exactly what she wanted with him. Nope, he hadn't minded that at all, and the thought of her breasts in the firelight was almost enough to make him pause, wait, take her back to his place before fucking her fast and hard with every ounce of pent-up need.

But he didn't want her to spend the ride down planning what she was going to do to him. He wanted her unscripted, unplanned. He wanted her now.

They were warm enough from the hike that they didn't have to get inside right away. And anyway, what he had in mind wouldn't take long. Austin slid off the front of the snowmobile, pulling Sam down with him.

"What are you—" she started, but when he turned her so she was facing the snowmobile, her back to him, it was clear. He pushed her shoulders down to bend her over the seat.

"Doesn't get more private than this," he grunted as he reached around and unzipped her ski pants, shimmying them over her ass. Sure, they were out in the open, exposed to the world. But there was no one around. No one to hear her moan his name.

She had on a sweet pair of wine-colored panties, and he

almost hated to slide them over her curves. But the sight of them pulled down around her thighs with the ski pants was even better. He unzipped his pants and pulled out his cock, throbbing already from the sight of her bare ass bent over the snowmobile, her clothes partway down. Her body was warm, heat radiating from exertion and desire. He slid a hand between her thighs and yes, she was wet, quivering, squirming to press her clit into his palm.

But he pulled away. He wanted her desperate, panting. He wanted her to need this fuck.

"I'll get cold," she moaned, holding fast to the seat of the snowmobile as she bent over. But she didn't make a move to stand. She didn't give any indication that she didn't like knowing he was getting off just watching her bend over for him.

Austin stepped closer. "I'll keep you warm," he whispered as he used his body to cover her, her ass pressed up against his cock.

"That's it, baby," he urged her, sliding his cock along the beautiful cleft.

"Please," she whimpered.

"Please what?"

"Please fuck me."

He pulled a condom out of his pocket. It had seemed silly at the time to bring one, but damn, was he glad for it now. He put it on and used his boot to kick out her legs wider. That alone made a groan escape from her lips, and he knew then that she wanted it like this, hard and fast, him taking her just how she'd taken him last night, without holding anything back.

He pressed the tip of his cock to her and she inched back, coaxing him in. He waited, filling her with anticipation, and then he plunged into her.

Sam gasped. Quickly the cry turned into a moan, low

and throaty, the sound of desire itself. Austin steadied himself with his hands on either side of her, gripping the seat of the snowmobile, and started to fuck her. The snowmobile rocked, but it was sturdy and stayed upright, no matter how hard Sam shook.

"Come," she commanded. "Come inside me. Please."

His only response was to hold on to her shoulders, pressing her down while giving him the leverage he needed to drive even deeper. Her cries carried across the open expanse, but he didn't care. There was no one around. And even if there were? He still wouldn't have cared. There was no longer anything in his world besides her body and the tension building inside him.

She could feel it, too. "Please," she said again, a gasp, her breath coming in short bursts as she held on. "I need you."

The three little words were like a jolt through his system, and he came as if on command, as if her words had unlocked something he couldn't contain. A force ripped through him and he let go with such completeness that he was shuddering afterward, slumped over her body, pressing her tight to him. He slid out of her and wrapped the condom in a tissue to throw away later. But when he pulled up his pants, he wished for a second that they'd actually waited and were inside so he could stay like that, holding her, feeling her heartbeat and the steady rise and fall of her breathing.

But they weren't inside, they were out in the snow and he'd just fucked her over the back of a snowmobile, and even though it had just happened it was hard to believe it was real and not some fantasy. Sam pulled up her pants and turned around, her cheeks flushed, lips raised in a coy half smile.

He reached for her, pulling her to him and kissing her because that was all he had when there weren't any words left to say.

"Damn," she finally whispered, eyes sparkling.

"We aren't done yet," he said, sliding his hands between her thighs.

She groaned, but in the end she shook her head. "How about that fireplace? Something warm for me to look forward to."

Austin drove the snowmobile back as fast as he dared. He could feel her clinging to him, rubbing against him, building the anticipation so that as soon as he flicked her clit with his fingers, his tongue, the tip of his cock, she would come.

His frustrations from that morning seemed like a lifetime away.

Chapter Fourteen

As soon as they started up Austin's truck, Sam pressed her fingertips to the heat vents to warm her hands. She didn't know how she felt about everything Austin had said, but at least she better understood where he was coming from. She was probably supposed to be thinking through how she could use that to convince him to sell, by showing him what wouldn't change and reassuring him of the measures Kane Enterprises was taking.

But mostly she was thinking how refreshing it was to talk to someone so passionate. So principled. Someone with more on his mind than the numbers in the latest contract or how he was going to look with Sam on his arm.

She was also thinking about how cold she was. The trip had been worth it, but damn did she need a hot shower and some of that cocoa Austin had brought her on the first day they met.

She needed that massage he'd been talking about, too. She was sore from skiing, hiking, fucking. Clenching to hold on. She was thrilled when they got back to Austin's and he called to make an appointment with his friend Claire for that afternoon.

"So she's good?" Sam asked as she took off her wet boots and tossed them by the door. "Will she take out my knots and not judge me for my horrible posture from hunching over the computer all day?"

Austin laughed. "Yes to the knots, but I can't promise anything about judgment. She's the nicest person you'll ever meet, though. Quieter than Mack, so don't worry, you'll be able to relax."

Sam stripped off her ski pants, jacket, and hat. "Should I have feelings about the nicest person I've ever met running her hands all over you every week?"

Austin backtracked from the kitchen, where he'd been getting food for Chloe, and put his arms around her. "Jealous, much?"

Sam let out a noise from the back of her throat, neither a yes nor a no. "Just curious."

Austin kissed her on each eyelid. She liked the brush of his scruff, the way he went for these small, sweet gestures to show he could touch her without it being 100 percent about getting in her pants. Although she was still waiting for that. The whole ride back she'd been hot and throbbing between her thighs, and now she hooked a leg around him. He ran a hand up her thigh, supporting her firmly under the ass.

"Claire is extremely professional," he said.

"That doesn't answer my question."

"And what is your question?" He bit her bottom lip.

Sam wasn't sure. Whether there was anything going on with Claire? Or whether she was in a position to know if there was anything going on with Claire to begin with?

She knew this was dangerous territory—she was supposed to be worrying about the sale she had to lock down, not whether she and Austin had a future. But when she pulled away, she caught sight of the bag with the gloves she'd bought him still sitting by the door and something clicked into place.

"Is that why you won't take the gloves?" she asked suddenly. "Because we're not…" She looked for the word but came up empty.

"Not what?" Austin prodded.

Sam shook her head. "Not whatever it is that we aren't."

Austin followed her gaze to the door and frowned. "I don't even know what that means."

"But it's a fair question."

"What are we, in court? What are you trying to ask?"

"How come you're gorgeous and funny and driven and hot as hell and have all these female friends you've mentioned, like Mack and Abbi and Claire, but apparently aren't sleeping with them?" she blurted out.

That hadn't been what she'd planned on saying. She wasn't sure what she'd planned on saying. *Here's why you need to sell to the Kanes* would have been a good start. Why couldn't she just do her job?

Austin wiped a hand over his mouth, but it didn't hide how red his face was. Was he laughing at her? Not single at all? Had he slept with every single one of his friends?

"Shit," Sam muttered when he didn't say anything. He had. He totally had.

"It's not what you're thinking," he said quickly, reaching for her. But she stepped away.

"What am I thinking." It wasn't a question. Her voice stayed flat.

He ducked his head. "You're thinking I sleep with everybody. You're thinking they're not really my friends. Trust me, Sam, there's nothing going on. I admit that Claire and I tried to make it work once, but it wasn't in the cards for us. It wasn't in the cards with any of them. It's a small town, and when I came here I needed friends more than lovers. I just—"

His hands dropped by his side. "I wasn't ready to commit."

Sam wasn't sure how to respond. That wasn't what she'd been expecting him to say. That wasn't even what she was looking for. Who said anything about commitment?

And yet, just how many lovers had he meant?

"So what are you looking for now?" she asked.

Austin looked at her plainly, more naked to her than when she'd seen him without clothes. "I don't know," he admitted.

She wished she hadn't said a thing. Why weren't they having sex now? Why hadn't he rushed her inside to tear her clothes off in front of the fire like last night? Why was this coming out wrong?

"I don't know why I asked that. That's not even something I'm worried about. Please, pretend I didn't say anything." Sam picked up the gloves from the floor and handed them to Austin. "And take the goddamn gloves." She cracked a smile. "If that's why you wouldn't take them, I'm telling you it's not a gesture that means anything. It's just me trying to beat out Claire for nicest person in the world."

Austin took the gloves and put them back by the door. "I know you didn't mean anything by it. But I still can't."

"But why not?" Sam was getting annoyed. "Your old gloves are falling apart, don't pretend nobody notices."

It was the exact wrong thing to say. His jaw tightened in anger. "I don't care whether anybody notices. This isn't about what people will think of me."

"I didn't mean it like that. You're twisting my words."

"You think what I have is shit, you think you have something better."

"They're just gloves, Austin. It's not a referendum on your fucking personality." She hadn't meant to curse, but he was being ridiculous. Her first instinct was to feel like she shouldn't have brought anything up, but that was bullshit. She had every right to ask who Claire was, who his friends were, and why Austin said and did the things he did. For the sake of her company—and also for herself.

But it hurt when he turned his back to her as though he couldn't even look at her when he said, "They're not just gloves."

"What?" Sam took a step toward him, her socks landing right in a puddle of melted snow. Could this get any worse? She honestly thought she hadn't heard him, but he turned and repeated it.

"They're not *just gloves*, okay? I know it sounds stupid to you. I don't expect you to understand and that's why I didn't say anything before. But since you won't let it go, they were a present from my uncle when I was accepted onto the U.S. Ski Team. You have this loving family and a father who clearly did everything for you and now you know I have nothing, okay? I have one pair of gloves that tells me somebody once gave a shit about me and I don't need you acting like I should throw that away."

He stormed off to the kitchen, pouring a glass of water and noisily drinking it down without offering any to her.

Sam stayed in the doorway and tried to think fast. "Austin, I'm sorry. I didn't know that and I wasn't trying to take anything away from you. I just wanted to do something nice."

She'd never seen his face look anything but gorgeous, but now he scowled, a hard, mean line to his mouth that made her recoil. Who was he? What was inside him that she didn't know? She couldn't begin to guess, but it was pissing her off that he wouldn't come out and tell her. How was she supposed to know the gloves were some sentimental thing? Why was she supposed to think he'd be anything but thrilled to have someone give him a new pair?

But it was obvious what was broken inside him. As soon as she asked herself the question, she knew.

"I'm sorry you fell, Austin," she said quietly. He looked at her from across the room, confusion etched on his brow.

"You don't know what you're talking about." His voice was cracked, defeated.

"I'm sorry that happened. I'm sorry you didn't get to go to the Olympics. I can't imagine the pain." She took a deep breath before he could interject and kept going. "But accidents happen. You said it yourself. You said it to Amelia, too. Hell, you even said it to me. Falling is how you know that you're pushing yourself, that you're learning. You told me you knew what you were getting into, that you accepted the consequences of engaging in a risky sport. Don't tell me that wasn't true."

Don't tell me you're not who I think you are, a voice inside her pleaded. Just another man who seemed like good news until you found out the ways he was broken inside.

Unfair, another voice countered. She was being so unfair.

But Austin was looking at her as though he'd never seen her before. Chloe's ears perked up, and the way the two of them stood there staring her down—Sam had never felt so unwelcome in all her life.

"Jesus Christ," Austin muttered, as though he couldn't believe what he was hearing.

"Am I wrong?"

"It wasn't a fucking accident, Sam. Do you hear me? You keep saying I fell, but I've never once told you that. You just assumed, like you assume I want new gloves, or that Amelia can't hack it, or that this Kane development is going to be so rosy for everyone so why don't I join in the fun. Does it ever occur to you to consider someone else's point of view? Someone who actually knows what they're living through?"

"I never—"

"I didn't fall," he said over her, loudly, and then again, "I didn't fall."

Sam stared at him. She didn't understand.

"Do you really want to know why I have these scars? Why I can't ski like I used to? Why I'm holed up here in the woods instead of a professional skier in Colorado, where I grew up, where I spent my entire life being coached by, led by, groomed by the world's best to be one of them?"

Sam stood there mutely. This was supposed to be fun, casual, a few nights of whatever it was before they both went back to their lives—a life in which she became the new owner of half his land. Not until now had she fully understood how serious this was, and how much more than just the sale she stood to lose.

Because here he was, spilling what he obviously didn't want to say and she didn't want to listen to, and it wasn't casual, it wasn't easy, it wasn't the kind of thing she could up and leave. She'd grown attached. She'd grown to care too much about him.

"What happened?" she whispered.

Austin's eyes were steely and hard. "My dad was beating on my mom because that's what he did, you know? No, wait." He shook his head. "I'd bet a million dollars you don't know. To you, that's what happens in movies, on TV. To those poor people who aren't fortunate enough to be you. But that's what he did, because he felt like it. Because he could. He was normally a belt kind of guy, but we were leaving through the garage and that's why he grabbed a hammer from the toolbox."

Sam's lips went numb. Her legs wouldn't move, no matter how much she wanted to cross the distance and lay her head on his chest.

Austin looked at a spot on the floor in front of her feet and continued as if in a trance.

"She was supposed to come stay with me in Park City. Imagine me taking my mom to the Olympics to watch me race. It was the proudest moment of my life. Not just that I was skiing, but that she would see.

"But she never showed up. My uncle couldn't get her to budge, my coach, no one. So I went back to get her and my dad, he just…" Austin ran a hand over his lips. "He was convinced she was leaving him, that I was coming to take her away for good." He laughed, a throttled, angry sound. "Who knows, maybe if I could have gotten her out of that house to go anywhere besides the grocery store, I would have. But I never got that far. He was going to kill her, Sam. I swear to God that was going to be the time when he finally killed my mother. So I stepped in."

Austin's eyes shot up and held her gaze, and now it was Sam who had to be strong and not look away even though his words were a weight around her neck, pulling her eyes to the floor, to her feet, her wet sock clinging to her toes.

"You saw the scars. Didn't you wonder why they're not in any kind of order? It's not just from surgery, Sam. Those are scars from the hammer. He didn't stop swinging until I'd passed out on the ground."

"Austin," Sam choked, but he waved his arm, dismissing her in a way that nobody did. Not when they knew they were in front of a Kane.

"He knew what was expected of me at the Olympics. There I was, nineteen years old, with a real chance to make something of myself. And if I did, I wouldn't be coming back to his shitty house in his shitty town to take his shitty abuse anymore. It's not just that he didn't want me to ski again. He didn't want me to be able to walk."

Sam felt her phone vibrate in her pocket with a text message. She couldn't think about work right now. Her stomach hurt. Her saliva was thick as paste. She wanted to tell Austin how sorry she was, how she'd never meant to assume.

She wanted to tell him, too, not to be angry with her. He'd

let her go on believing one version of events when he could have corrected her at any point. So why was he yelling like this was her fault?

But she was in no position to talk to him about honesty. Hadn't she done the same thing, putting forward one version of herself, keeping the ugly truths safely out of view? Before she could open her mouth, her phone vibrated again. This time, it didn't stop—not a text message, but a call.

She silenced it without seeing who it was. She didn't want Austin thinking she always put her job first, attached to that phone like it was a third person forever in the room. But he frowned, like he thought it anyway.

Before he could open his mouth, his home phone started to ring, the sudden noise cutting through the silence between them. It rang three, four, five times, then clicked over to voicemail, or else the person hung up.

Sam was about to say something—to try to break the tension by commenting what a strange coincidence that was—when Austin's cell phone started ringing. It was set to "Ode to Joy" and was way too loud, sitting on a table by the door where he must have left it when they'd gone out.

For a second neither of them moved. Then Austin went past her to pick up the phone. He looked at it for a second, and Sam got the feeling he didn't recognize the number. She thought he'd ignore it—didn't he say he barely used the thing? But it was too much of a coincidence, those calls to them both in a row. He flipped it open and said hello.

Sam was completely outside herself. It was as though she was standing on the sidewalk and watching a stranger's house burn down, not realizing it was her own house, her own life, being sent up in flames. But of course she knew. From somewhere in the back of her mind, the wolf, the bitch, snidely asked how long she'd expected to keep up this charade.

Austin frowned, looked away, and said, "How did you get

my number?"

Before he could hear the answer, she plucked the phone out of his hands. "Steven, it's Sam. Tell the board to cool it. I'll call you back."

She hung up the phone, handed it to Austin, and steeled herself to face what she had done.

Chapter Fifteen

"How did you know who that was?"

It surprised him how quiet his voice was. How level. How cold. How could he speak to Sam in a voice that cold?

But it wasn't Sam. That woman was a fiction, a lie. She might as well not exist.

"Please," she said, and although she was trying to sound in command, he could sense the desperation. "Please, Austin. Let me explain."

But there was nothing to explain. He got it now—how she was glued to her phone but never let him see what she was working on, how she kept pressing him about the deal so she could worm her way in. She hadn't even told him her last name. He'd fallen for a woman without even asking her last name.

"You're Samantha Kane," he said. The words cut like glass in his mouth. Even though he knew it was true, it still hit him like a fall on hard snow when she said yes.

"But that doesn't matter," she said quickly. "That doesn't change how I feel."

"It certainly changes how *I* feel."

She flinched as though surprised by how angry he was. Was she kidding? Was she completely insane?

"You have to believe me, Austin," she pleaded. "I never meant for you to find out like this."

He couldn't believe she had the gall to say that, to stand there and defend herself to him. "You never meant for me to find out at all. All you've done this whole time is lie."

"No. I never—"

"You looked me in the eyes and listened when I talked about the Kanes and the land and the sale and *everything* and you smiled and nodded and asked bland little questions like 'What would you do to Gold Mountain if you could do anything here?' And the whole time you've been laughing your head off at how stupid I am, just some small-town hick you can manipulate into giving you what you want."

His face burned in shame at how he'd been played.

"That's not what happened," Sam said, but he wrenched away when she reached for him. He couldn't bear to let her touch him anymore. She held up her hands, clearly stung, but he didn't care.

"Maybe it started that way," she said. "Maybe I thought when I first met you that I could use what I learned for the sale. But then I got to know you, and I—"

She'd been trying to keep her voice level, but it broke and she couldn't go on.

"And you *what*? Thought if you pity fucked me a few times, I'd give you my house, too?"

She took a breath, steadying herself. "And I found myself falling in love with you."

No. *No.* That was too much. "You don't get to say that."

"It's true."

He clenched his jaw so hard he thought his teeth might crack. "It's *bullshit*. You don't get to screw me for a few days and make me think that meant something to you, and then brag to your fucking board and your fucking assistant and your shareholders or whoever else you serve that you got the thing you came here for."

"That's not what happened!"

"Well, I guess it doesn't matter now, does it? Considering I can't trust a damn thing you say." He laughed, a sound that wasn't like laughter at all.

"Austin, you have to believe me. I've risked everything for you—my job, this sale, the whole future of my father's project. There are people on my board that want to replace me if I can't make this deal go through. And the Hendersons aren't going to sign if I make them keep waiting. I told Steven I'd met with you in order to give us more time. I shouldn't have done it, I know that, but all I've wanted ever since I set foot in Gold Mountain was to spend more time with you."

"So you could manipulate me."

"So I could be with you without this awful business deal defining us. I've put everything on hold—"

"I didn't ask you to do that."

"Everything on hold to be with you," she plowed on, as though his perspective didn't matter. As though she thought she could handle this the way she probably handled everything in her office, by being firm and unwavering, the lone voice in charge, the one to whom everybody caved.

But this wasn't her office, and he wasn't going to let her walk away unscathed.

"You made me think you were here to ski," he said. "You said you wanted to remember your dad. Such a touching family legacy that's turned out to be, daddy and daughter stripping half the state, making money hand over fist."

Her nostrils flared. "Don't you dare bring my father into this," she said in a voice so laced with anger it was almost animal.

"I told you *everything*," he cried, sweeping his arm to take in the room, his home, the woods beyond the back door.

"I told you about my father, my mother, the truth about my injury—things I barely even tell my best friends." Then he dropped his hand with a shrug. "But maybe this is just what you do, *Samantha*. Maybe this is what it means to be some gazillionaire executive with a stack of lawyers at your back. You come into a place and you get people to spill their guts to you, but you don't care, you already have all the money, the power. You get to play around with the regular folk and in the end you still get everything you want."

She shook her head furiously. "I never made you tell me anything. And the fact that you don't share this kind of stuff with your friends—I don't know what to tell you, but none of that's on me. And you didn't tell me about your parents. You yelled at me, Austin, and now it's awfully convenient that this has come up so you can yell at me some more."

That was too much. Like it was his fault Sam had decided to play this prank and gotten caught. Like he was to blame for daring to be upset with her.

"When were you even going to tell me?" he asked her, genuinely wanting to know. "Or were you just going to leave me hanging and then send someone in your stead like nothing happened?"

There was a pause, and Austin realized he'd hit a nerve. "I don't know," Sam said. But her voice was quiet, different. Far more pained.

"I don't know, okay?" She started to cry. "I didn't have a plan, and I *always* have a plan. Don't you know that about me? I always have a plan, and then you came along and suddenly I had no idea what to do."

He could almost do it. Take her in his arms, kiss her forehead, tell her it would be okay. Maybe this was the way he could keep his land, by convincing Sam she cared too much for him to pressure him to sell.

But that was a Kane way of thinking, and it disgusted him

that such a thing had crossed his mind. Sam had played him, pure and simple. There was nothing else for either of them to explain.

"I know what you should do," he said.

"What?" She looked at him hopefully.

"First thing is to get your boots on. Next is to get in the truck. You'll have a nice long drive to Seattle to work out what to do after that."

"No," Sam said, shaking her head. "I'm not leaving like this. Who I am, where I work—it doesn't have to change anything if we don't want it to."

He stared at her like he'd never seen her before. Her, whose body he'd gazed at, ravaged, held. He'd felt so close to her. It occurred to him he might never feel that close to anyone again.

And then he said the cruelest words he could think of, the ones that would cut her as much as she'd done to him. "I want it to."

They drove to the Dipper in silence. She tried, once, to ask if there was anything she could do to make it better. But the fact that she thought what she'd done was forgivable only showed how different they were.

He thought she might turn around before she got in her car, try one last time. But nothing she could say would change his mind—about their relationship, or the sale.

He drove home gripping the steering wheel until his knuckles turned white. The shame in him was all-consuming, a fire that melted everything inside him down to thick black sludge. He didn't usually let Chloe up on the furniture, but when he got home he begged her to sit beside him. He felt her weight against him, the warmth of her breathing. Her unconditional love. They gazed at the cold, soot-covered fireplace. He couldn't even bear to get up and bring in the wood.

Chapter Sixteen

Sam cried as she brushed snow off her car. She'd known the end was inevitable. But she'd only considered it happening on her terms. *She'd* set the agenda, *she'd* make the deal, *she'd* be the one to walk away. She'd only ever imagined herself calling the shots—just like she always did.

She got inside the car, teeth chattering, and cranked the heat, waiting for the ice on the windshield to melt. She was shivering, crying, and angry. She'd fucked up, she knew that completely. But she wasn't the only one who'd been lying. It was all a sham, a goddamn lie. The whole front he'd presented, as though he were happy with his life.

And the final cherry on top of her shit sundae? She hadn't even gotten off after he did. Her legs felt sticky. As she pulled out of the parking lot, she felt a sourness resembling shame.

But she wasn't going to lose everything she'd worked for. She'd come here for a reason. It was time to remember what that was.

Set a plan and follow it, her father would say. Take one step, and the next will follow.

There was only one move left she could think of. She was going to go to her hotel and pack her things. Then it was time to get out of this town.

As Steven's call had reminded her, she'd already stayed for too long.

• • •

For the first time ever, Austin was late to practice.

"Ooh, too much time with *Sam*?" Kelsey sang when he finally showed up in the lodge.

"Let's get to work," he said.

Kelsey smacked her gum loudly. "Aw, come on, Austin. Not even any juicy details?" The girls snickered. It was obvious they'd been talking about him the whole time they'd been standing around.

He got close to her face. "It's Coach, not Austin. And spit out your gum." He pointed to a trash can. "I've been going too easy on you. All of you." He stared each of them down—especially Amelia. "Nothing about finals is guaranteed. You make it because you work hard. If you don't want to put in the work, save me the trouble and go home."

He never spoke like this, his voice clipped, his eyes cold. The girls shrank away.

"Now!" he barked at Kelsey. She flinched in surprise.

"Fuck you, too, *Coach*," Kelsey muttered under her breath as she slumped over to the trash. Austin talked right over her, coming up with the toughest sequence he could think of for the day's lesson.

"And anyone who drops a ski on the balance runs is doing sprints when we get back," he added. "Am I clear?"

He'd never heard so much complaining.

"Guess he got dumped," Kelsey grumbled as they lined up for the lift.

Austin kept his face stony, as though he'd heard nothing. Why should he care what a bunch of kids said? Why care what anyone said? He had his life, his friends, his dog, his routine. He'd let himself get too wrapped up in some stranger he'd never expected to stick around anyway, and now he'd learned his lesson. No more distractions. No more Sam.

The girls started running their drills, but it was terrible. The team was angry. Austin kept snapping at them, making everything worse. He knew the times he expected from them were out of reach for anyone but Amelia, but even she kept falling short.

When she got to the bottom of the trail, he pulled her aside.

"Come on," he shouted. "What's going on out there? Your pole touches are sloppy, your pivot slips aren't low enough, and you're still not forward on the first gate. Stop holding back and get to work!"

"It's *practice*," Amelia protested. "I wasn't treating it like a real race."

"When *are* you going to treat this like a real race?" He got up in her face, making sure she knew how serious he was. "If you don't do the work now, you'll never be ready, and I can guarantee that spot in Utah will go to someone who is."

Amelia's eyes widened, then rimmed with red. He knew he was being harsh, but didn't she get it? This wasn't some practice run before her real life got started. This was it, the only shot she had. He didn't want her to lose it.

"In case you haven't noticed," she said through clenched teeth, "I'm trying."

"Well, try harder."

"I *am*," she repeated. "But I guess nothing I do is good enough for you. Looks like you're just going to have to get used to being disappointed."

She said it with a scowl, and Austin might have let it

go—he had the rest of the team to attend to—but he was so stunned, it cut through the fog that had enveloped him ever since he'd picked up the phone and heard the words, "This is Steven Park."

"What are you talking about?"

"Seriously? It's like if I don't ski hard enough you'll be pissed, but if I ski any harder I'll blow out and then I really *will* break my nose."

"I can't believe you think that." All the anger melted out of him like snow trickling into a stream. "I can't believe you think I could be disappointed in you."

A tear slid down her lashes and onto her cheek. "Of course you're going to be disappointed. I'm, like, basically guaranteed to let you down. You have this idea that if we work hard enough, we can have anything."

"But you can," he said, not understanding. "Whatever it is you want, each of you on the team, I want you to know you can get it."

"But then what if I bomb the finals and this Utah thing doesn't work out? What if I fall or miss a gate or am a tenth of a second too late? That must mean I didn't work hard enough, I didn't really want it, it's all my fault." Her eyes widened as imaginary disasters danced in her mind.

"That's not at *all* what I mean," Austin said in alarm. "Are you stressed about the finals? I know you've got this. Everything's going to be fine."

"But what if it doesn't work the way you think it will? What if I try my hardest and I'm *still* not good enough? What if I never wind up being as good as you?"

She swallowed, waiting for him to assure her the world still worked in the neat little ways he said it did: set your eye on a goal, follow through, complete it as planned.

But he couldn't. Because Amelia was right.

"Okay," he said. "You want me to be honest?"

She nodded.

"It might not happen. It might all fuck up—I mean mess up," he said quickly, and she snickered and rolled her eyes, "in a spectacular way." He tapped his pole to his knee. "I've had some experience with that."

"So?" she said quietly. "What if that happens to me?"

"I can guarantee what happened to my knee will never in a million years happen to you," he said firmly. "And some day that's not today, I'll tell you how I know that. But yeah, something else might happen. There's always a chance you won't make it as far as I think. But that doesn't mean it's your fault. And it certainly doesn't mean I'll think any less of you. If things don't go as planned, we'll come up with a new plan. Okay?"

She nodded, wiping her eyes. "Okay."

"Now get out of here. The rest of the team is leaving us in the dust."

Amelia bit her lip, like there was one last thing she wanted to say.

"What?" he asked. "Out with it."

"Did you and Sam have a fight? Is that why you're so pissy today?"

Why couldn't he coach five-year-olds instead? Or adults. People who got that life was complicated and there were some things you couldn't come back from, situations where you tried and tried to do everything right and still it wound up all wrong.

"Mind your own business or I'll make you run stairs in the gym after practice," he said gruffly.

"You should just tell her you're sorry and make up. She's nice and gorgeous and you should see the way she looked at you when you guys met. Seriously." She eyed him solemnly. "Don't do that thing guys do when they get all dumb and won't talk."

"Amelia, I know you're trying to tell me I'm pushing you too hard, but I swear to God—"

"I know, I know, you'll make me run stairs." She used her poles to push away from him and skated over to the lift.

"And tell the girls to stop gossiping!" he shouted after her, even though he knew it was hopeless.

But at least she was laughing, which hopefully meant she didn't think he was a total asshole for the way he'd been acting at practice. And that she wouldn't keep psyching herself out on these runs.

It wasn't like he'd talk about his dating life with his team, but he wished it were as simple as Amelia said. He wished he'd had a regular fight with Sam, the kind where people talked afterward and found a resolution.

This was different. There'd be no more talking to Sam— or Ms. Kane, he corrected himself in his mind, and the surge of anger he'd almost forgotten in his concern for Amelia all came flooding back.

Didn't Amelia get it? He didn't *want* her to be like him. That was the whole point. He didn't want her to fail.

He wanted everything to work out the way it was supposed to—no slipups, no surprises, nothing unplanned.

Only maybe, when he put it like that, the kid had a point.

He tried to focus on the rest of practice, but his head felt like it was a thousand pounds. His jaw hurt from clenching it so tight. He realized as he sat on the chairlift that he'd been peeling strips of old tape off his gloves.

In the end, he let them go early. Everyone was too tired to be good for much, anyway.

Chapter Seventeen

Sam lay on her stomach, enveloped in warmth. The sheets were soft, the lighting dim, a faint citrus smell drifting through the room. She'd been so anxious to leave after her fight with Austin, and then she remembered. Austin had scheduled her a massage with his friend.

His friend who was apparently an ex, which might have been enough to send Sam screaming except no way was she slinking away with her tail between her legs. She wanted a massage, she had an appointment for a massage, so damn it, she was getting her massage. It wasn't like she could get away with not showing her face here again, so she'd better start learning to own it.

Sam looked up Claire's business on her phone and drove over. The woman who greeted her was tall, lithe as a dancer, and everything about her radiated calm. Sam was glad she'd taken the time to dab makeup under her eyes in the car to hide the puffiness from crying. She tried to hold her head high as she shook Austin's ex's hand.

But if Claire had any inkling who Sam had briefly been in

Austin's life, or cared one way or another, she didn't give any indication. "So you're Austin's friend," she said kindly, inviting Sam in. Sam wished she could be as collected. As soon as Claire led her into the massage room and left her to change, she practically collapsed.

Claire warmed oils between her palms and slid her hands down Sam's back. Her fingers were capable and strong. Sam let out a groan.

"Let me guess," Claire said. "You sit at a desk all day."

"Is it that obvious?" Sam asked as Claire's fingers found the place between her shoulder blades that always hurt.

"You're completely locked up in here. I barely feel any give."

Sam grunted. It was ironic to hear herself described as ungiving when the gift of those stupid gloves had played no small role in this mess.

"Too hard?" Claire asked, pausing.

"No," Sam said quickly. "The harder the better." No release without pain.

She took deep breaths, exhaling as Claire's fingers dug in. It was a welcome distraction to focus on the soreness in her body instead of the soreness in her heart, but the silence didn't last long.

"What brings you to Gold Mountain?" Claire asked as she worked.

"A few days of skiing," Sam said, trying to keep her voice casual. "Get a little break from Seattle."

"Give those shoulders a rest."

"The skiing probably doesn't help. All that poling." She didn't explain exactly why she'd used her ski poles so much, getting across to Austin's secret shelter. And then—was it just that morning?—she'd strained her arms holding onto the snowmobile for her dear life. She felt tears welling up and was glad her face was down so Claire couldn't see.

"I'll work on your legs next," Claire promised. "I'm sure they're sore from the slopes."

"You must see a lot of that around here," she said, trying not to sniffle.

"That's what I do for Austin."

"Uh-huh." A simple comment, no emotion involved. No indication that he'd just had her bent over a snowmobile, or on his couch, or in an old mining shelter in the middle of the mountains. No sign that she'd spent all night wrapped in his arms. And certainly no hint at what they'd just yelled at each other before he kicked her out.

Sam hoped that would be it for chitchat about Austin. Weren't these things more relaxing when they were quiet? But clearly Claire could work and talk, because as she folded the top sheet down to draw her palms along the muscles hugging Sam's spine, she asked, "So how long have you known Austin? I never heard him mention a Seattle friend."

Sam nearly choked as Claire pressed into her lower back.

"Water?" Claire asked, concerned.

"No, I'm fine. Um, Austin and I just met, actually. Up here. I don't really know him that well." That was certainly the truth.

"Oh," Claire said, a long sound to accompany the slide of her hands. "I'm sorry, I just assumed."

"We met skiing, and then ran into each other again at Mack Daddy's."

Claire laughed. "Nice, I see you've got the lingo down."

"When in Rome."

"I'm glad he recommended you come. I'm just surprised— he made it sound on the phone like he'd known you for longer." Claire tucked the sheet up over Sam's shoulders and helped her roll over under it, so she was lying on her back. With quick precision Claire folded the bottom of the sheet up to her thighs and walked around the table to work on her legs.

"He said to be sure you got the best."

"Yeah, I don't know," Sam said absently, her eyes on the ceiling, trying to take those big, long breaths that were supposed to be calming but always made her feel like she wasn't getting enough air.

"Oh," Claire said, standing over her. And then, "I'm so sorry, I'm being an idiot. I didn't mean to…" She ducked her head and began working on Sam's legs. Her hands were strong, the massage finely calibrated to knead the fibers where Sam was sorest.

"It's okay," Sam assured her. Claire continued to work in silence, obviously embarrassed. The pressure from her fingers was pure bliss, and Sam relaxed into it. Everything in her was loosening, her shoulders and neck having given up the tension they'd been holding onto. Maybe that was why the next words slipped out before she could stop them. "It seemed like we might have had a thing, but it looks like not."

She wondered if she sensed a tightening in Claire's hands or if she was making it up. "What happened?" Claire asked.

Sam snorted. "It started when I bought him a pair of gloves."

She thought Claire would laugh, or at least require more explanation, but instead she stopped her work on Sam's calf and stared at her. "You've known him for how long and were going to get him to give up that ratty pair?"

"Apparently everyone but me knows they're a thing."

"What did he say when you gave them to him?" Claire went back to work.

"That he couldn't take them."

Claire made a sound like *mmm-hmm* between her teeth. And since Sam was spread out on the table, her limbs loose as jelly, she said, "The first time. The second time I told him to take them he said I didn't understand anything and thought I was better than him."

"I'm impressed you got as far as that. Austin is the hardest person to do anything for. It freaks him out, like he might actually wind up getting close to someone."

"He certainly didn't make it sound like he was in danger of getting too close to me," Sam grumbled.

Claire smiled. "That's how you know you got under his skin."

"What is this, middle school?" She tried to put some bite into her voice, but it didn't work. Another tear streaked down her cheek. Everything she'd told herself about one night with Austin seemed so foolish now. How could she have kidded herself that she'd be able to get her fix and then be done, back to business as usual as though nothing had changed?

Claire got up and passed her a tissue. Gently she said, "I wondered if everything was okay when you came in."

So she'd known Sam had been crying. It sent a stab through Sam's chest to be so vulnerable in front of a stranger, but this wasn't the office, there wasn't some kind of strength test she had to pass. No one here was expecting her to be anyone other than some woman on vacation, tired, sore, here for a few days and then gone. The next time they saw her she'd be in a suit with a barrage of publicists managing her every move. That she'd once cried on a massage table wouldn't mean a thing.

"I feel so stupid," Sam said, blowing her nose. "I thought it was just some accident and then—"

"Wait," Claire interrupted her. "He told you that? I thought this was just about the gloves."

"'Told' may be the wrong word. There was quite a bit of yelling involved. It was the most awful thing I've ever heard, but it wasn't even the hammer. Believe it or not, I can handle the hammer. I just didn't expect him to get so mad at me." Suddenly she thought of something and winced. "Please tell me you knew that already. Please tell me I didn't just say something else I shouldn't have."

"Don't worry," Claire said. "I knew. But can you believe I worked on Austin for four years before he finally stopped talking vaguely about 'the accident' and finally came out with the truth? That's four years he came in once a week, every Monday, for me to work on his knee. It was always a puzzle to me how he'd managed to get scar tissue where he has it. I'm not saying Austin's right, just that it took him forever to open up to me. And that was on top of me complaining that I couldn't help him get over an injury if I didn't know what the injury was."

She bent Sam's leg up, rotated it in her hip socket, and placed it down again, repeating with the other leg. The simple motion, loosening her hips, felt so good Sam asked her to do it again.

"I'm not sure what happened counted as opening up," she said.

"Still, I'm impressed he said anything at all."

"It doesn't matter. He hates me now. He thinks I'm, I don't know, naive."

"It's not hate."

"Trust me, it is." Sam sighed. And then, because it was time to stop playing the game that had gotten her nowhere, she told Claire the rest of the story—the part where Austin wasn't to blame, but her.

"What I just said—the gloves, the accident—that all happened. And you're right, if it had just been that, I might believe there'd still be a chance. But I'm not being fair, the way I'm describing it. It's not the only thing that happened."

"Tell me," Claire said gently. "I'm not going to judge."

Sam let out a long exhale. "You should. Austin has every right to."

Claire brought her legs back down and began pushing on the tops of her ankles. The pressure was strange, but when she let up, Sam could feel it. The line down the front of her legs felt open, stretched.

She wasn't pushing Sam to say anything. She was simply giving her the space to get there on her own. When Steven called, Sam had been forced to confess. This time, it was up to her.

"Austin didn't tell you my full name when he booked the appointment. I didn't put it on the intake sheet, either." Her voice was barely a whisper, but in the quiet room it felt too loud. *You don't have to do this*, she reminded herself.

But she did.

"That's okay," Claire said, marching a sweet-sore line of pressure up her shins.

"He didn't tell you because he didn't know it."

Claire took her hands off Sam. Sam felt the absence immediately and regretted what she'd said. She wasn't thinking properly. She was going to make everything worse.

Claire was friends with Austin. She'd probably spent countless nights hanging out with Mack and Connor at the Dipper, downing beers and going on about those awful Kanes. Claire wasn't going to tell her this wasn't her fault. Claire was going to throw Sam's clothes at her and tell her to get out.

"So, what's your name?" Claire asked. She said it like she was asking a new patient where they'd grown up, or what they did for a living—just a way of making conversation. But she wasn't touching Sam. It was clear the massage had stopped.

Sam took a deep breath and forced out the answer. "Samantha Kane," she said, only it didn't come out the way she usually said it, strong and proud. For the first time in her life, she was ashamed of the person she'd become.

Claire didn't say anything. Sam stared at the ceiling, a tear trickling down her temple. When she dared to tilt her head to look over, Claire was staring at her. "Seriously?"

"The one and only." Sam sighed and went back to her

ceiling view. "Only I managed to keep that minor detail from Austin until this afternoon."

"Well, *shit*." Claire used a towel to wipe massage oils off her fingers.

"I can go," Sam said, starting to shift. "I'm sorry, I know I'm not welcome here. I shouldn't have wasted your time. Or his."

"Lie down, Sam. I still have to do your head. I'm afraid if I let you out of here carrying this much tension, you're going to explode."

Sam did as she was told. As Claire pressed her fingertips to Sam's temples, Sam told her everything. About how she'd come to Gold Mountain wanting one thing, only to find something else altogether.

"But now it's too late. I know we'd never be able to make it work anyway. But I made it so much worse by pretending. I should have been up front from the beginning. Even if it meant I couldn't have him at all."

Claire sighed and handed Sam another tissue. "I don't know if Austin told you this, but he and I dated for two and a half seconds, ages ago. Don't worry," she added quickly. "I think he's wonderful, but we're better as friends. I have a daughter, Maya, and I love her to pieces, but having a four-year-old isn't great for my social life. Trust me when I say you have nothing to worry about."

"Thanks, I believe you. But the real reason I have nothing to worry about is because there is no me and Austin. It's been three days. I live in Seattle. He hates me. *I* hate me. It's really not a thing."

"What I was going to say is that I know Austin pretty well. I know how tight-lipped and impossible he can be." She laughed wryly. "The fact that you've been to his house, that you know things he barely shares with anyone—you may have started this thinking there'd be no strings attached, but it's clear that wasn't true."

"If only that meant anything," Sam said. She closed her eyes, trying to let the feeling of Claire's hands transport her, but it was hard to feel relaxed anymore when all she wanted was to curl up and cry.

"Of course it does. Things changed for you. No matter what happens with Austin, you can't deny that you're leaving Gold Mountain different than when you came."

The evidence that Claire was right was there in the quickly mounting pile of tissues balled in Sam's fist. But even though Sam had to admit that yes, she *had* changed, no one could do a complete 360. She was still her. Samantha Kane.

What was more, she still *wanted* to be her. Sam had pretended she could divide herself into two parts, the one she was with Austin and the one coming for his land. But they were the same Samantha Kane, just as he was the Austin she'd known in person and the Mr. Reede who'd once been nothing to her but a name on a page.

"I just can't imagine going back to Seattle as though none of this happened," Sam said with a sigh.

"So don't."

"What do you mean?"

"Don't go back to Seattle as though nothing happened. Just because it didn't work—because you're too different, or can't be the people you need, or you've simply hurt each other too much—doesn't mean you don't have a choice. We always have a choice. You don't have to pretend nothing happened here. Who knows," she added. "It may make you feel better if you have to come back for work some time."

Sam lay on the table in the dark for a long time after Claire left, feeling the quiet, floating sensation of her body after the massage. She felt slippery, soft, like her limbs were no longer attached. The massage hurt but in a good way, the pain pushing out the underlying soreness, leaving her tender and new.

She wasn't exactly sure what Claire had meant by saying Sam had a choice. It wasn't like there was anything left she could do. But the words stayed with her as she went back to her car and asked herself, *what next?*

Chapter Eighteen

"You drinking that beer or just looking at it?" Mack shot Austin a look as she ran a cloth over the surface of the bar.

Austin took a halfhearted sip.

"What's wrong with you, anyway? Where's that Sam girl? I liked her—even if she has no taste in burgers." Mack stopped cleaning and frowned at him. "Don't tell me you scared her away."

"Believe it or not, I wasn't the asshole this time," Austin said glumly, and Mack raised an eyebrow.

"Shit, Austin, I was just kidding." She rapped on the door to the kitchen to get Connor's attention. "I'd pour you another beer, but you're barely making it through that."

"I don't want anything." Austin stared into the glass. "I just want to sit here and feel like an idiot."

It beat feeling like an idiot at home, which was what he'd been doing, staring into the ashes of the fireplace and thinking how blind he'd been.

Then he'd discovered an even better way to torture himself. A Google image search for Samantha Kane yielded hundreds of photos. He'd scrolled endlessly through a repeating loop of her face. Sam smiling for the cameras. Sam looking stern walking out of the Kane offices with an entourage in tow. Sam standing behind a podium, bathed in stage light.

Sure, he'd read the news stories about the company, the turnover from father to daughter. He and his friends talked plenty about Kane's plans to transform Gold Mountain into a massive resort. But he'd never looked closely enough at her picture to imprint her face in his mind. He thought of everything Sam—no, *Samantha*—had said about her father, her grief, and how much she seemed to love the places he took her in the snow. It was impossible to put together the heartfelt person he'd met with the impersonal face looking out from his screen.

He'd slammed the computer closed, heart pounding, and booked it over to Mack Daddy's. At least there he had company, even if he wasn't much for talking.

Although, he was beginning to think it would have been better to stay home alone. Mack was darting him worried looks, Connor was calling for someone to cover him, and he was in the process of telling them both to leave him alone when Claire slammed down on a bar stool next to him and said, "Don't even think about doing that thing I know you're doing."

"Uh, nice to see you, too. It's been a while. How's Maya?"

"I put Abbi on emergency babysitting detail so I could come over here."

"How'd you know I'd be here?"

"Because there are so many other places any of us go when a relationship ends?"

Austin felt three faces looking way too intently at him.

"It wasn't a relationship," he told Claire. "I'll be fine."

"Sure," Claire said. "If you insist. But you should at least keep the gloves."

He spun on the bar stool. "How'd you know about that?"

"She came to see me." Mack poured a glass of wine, and Claire took a sip like Austin wasn't about to jump out of his seat, wanting to know every detail about where Sam had been, what she'd said, what Claire thought of her. "That massage, you know."

"I can't believe she stayed for it."

"I can't believe you want to return them."

"Wait—she got you a new pair of gloves?" Mack looked from Austin to Claire and back again. "*You?* That's, like, serious." She sounded impressed.

"This is a lot more complicated than a pair of gloves, you guys," Austin said before they could all gang up on him.

"She told me who she is," Claire said.

That got Austin's attention.

And everyone else's. "Who is she?" Mack asked eagerly.

Claire glanced at Austin. He gestured for her to go ahead and say it. He couldn't get the words out without them sticking in his throat.

"Samantha Kane," Claire whispered.

Mack's mouth froze in an O. Even Connor let out a "holy shit." Austin groaned and covered his face in his hands.

"So now you all know and we can move on to pretending this never happened."

"I don't get it," Mack said. "How on earth did you fuck *Samantha Kane*?" Austin glared at her, and she held up her hands. "I'm just saying."

"I didn't know she was Samantha Kane when I was—" *fucking her*, he almost said but couldn't. "With her," he decided, since it wasn't like they'd had sex one time and that was it. No—regardless of how he'd insisted it wasn't a relationship, he'd taken her to the shelter, and up to the peak, and said those things to her about the metal that flashed in his dreams, the cries that filled his mind in the night.

Once again, it hit him how he'd been played. He'd felt that close to her, too close to brush it off as nothing. And yet he hadn't even known who she was.

"So she lied to you." Mack refilled Austin's glass and handed it back to him. "On the house," she added. "That fucking bitch."

Connor made a face. "That seems a little harsh. She didn't tell him the truth, yeah. But that's not the same as lying."

Mack raised an eyebrow at him. "Remind me never, ever to date you."

"I'm just saying. We weren't there. We don't know her the way Austin does."

"Aren't you listening?" Austin interjected. "That's the whole point. *I* don't know her, either."

"It's not like you slept with an ax murderer."

Mack rolled her eyes. "I love how Connor thinks truthfulness about her basic identity and/or her motivation in completely fucking Austin over are irrelevant here."

"Yeah," Claire said. "But what about the fact that Sam *likes* him?"

"Don't sound so shocked," Austin grumbled.

"I just mean that even though this started one way, something changed for her. She was crying on that massage table, Austin. She didn't get those gloves for you to buy you out. And she didn't press you about your life so she'd have leverage. She was falling in love with you. And you—" She threw up her hands. "You were *you*, which means you showed her the time of her life and then started pushing her away even before you knew you had an ironclad excuse to get her out of your life."

"Now that," Austin said, raising his glass to clink it with hers, "is the biggest load of bullshit I've heard all week. And believe me when I say I've heard a lot."

Claire slid off her stool. "I'm just saying. You guys

obviously connected in a real way or neither of you would be this upset. And she's obviously more than just some CEO or you wouldn't have had anything to connect over in the first place. You think you have everything planned out, like God forbid you let anyone into your life to shake things up, but think about it, Austin. Just—don't be so quick to throw this one away."

She gave Austin a hug. "And now I've got to go pick up my evidence that I know all about plans going awry." She laughed at herself as Mack told her to bring Maya next time, she'd have a hot chocolate waiting for her with extra whipped cream.

Claire left, and Mack refilled Austin's glass. Connor had to head back into the kitchen, but it wasn't long before he came back with a plate loaded with way too much food.

"Roast chicken, mashed potatoes, and those lemony greens I know you like," he announced.

"You don't have to do this," Austin said.

"Women may love your independent broody thing, but someone's got to make sure you eat. Plus you need something to soak up the booze Mack is plying you with."

"She sure is a good friend," Austin said with a grin.

Connor paused for a moment, and Austin thought he was going to go back to the kitchen. But Connor leaned his elbows on the bar and sighed. "You shouldn't feel bad. If you do—you shouldn't. If you hate her, that's fine. But you don't *have* to, you know?"

"I'm not sure what the other options are. It's not like I could ever actually date her at this point."

"Neutral indifference? Fond memory? Thing of the past you never dwell on again?"

Austin laughed. "You're good at this."

"Dude. We all have skeletons. Not all of them are quite as, uh, high profile as yours. But don't you remember that snowboarder with the pigtails who kept hanging around the bar that time?"

"Of course. Everyone else knew that was a no-fly zone. But no, you were the one who had to go for it." Austin rolled his eyes.

"How was I supposed to know she'd never want to leave?"

"Is this supposed to be some kind of helpful analogy?"

"I'm just saying. We all do things that aren't the world's best ideas. We all get involved with people before we fully know them. Sometimes it's for the better, sometimes it's not. And yet, miraculously, the world goes on."

He patted Austin on the shoulder and went back to work. Austin nodded, thanking him for the food, the advice, the company. But secretly, his insides wrenched at what Connor said.

He knew what his friend meant. This was one blip. It didn't have to define him or change his life forever.

But what if he didn't want the world to go on as usual? What if he'd *liked* the way things had started to change when Sam came into his life? He thought about Amelia, her eyes rimmed with red as she confessed her fears to Austin—that she wouldn't be good enough for him. That she'd try her best and still fall short.

Did he expect too much? Was he so rooted to one way of doing things, he couldn't imagine trying anything else?

Of course he knew plans changed. The very fact that he was in Gold Mountain and not a pro skier in Colorado was proof. And yet how much more strongly did he cling to his home, his life, as a result? How much harder had that made it for him to embrace anything unexpected, where he couldn't plan the outcome? Where he had no idea what came next.

"Hey, Mack," he called, and she left a group of customers and came over to him.

"Another one?" she asked, but Austin said no. He needed

to keep his head screwed on now.

"Do you guys have a fax machine here?"

"There's one in the office. Why?"

"Can you give me the number? I might want to use it."

"Sure," she said and wrote it down. "What do you need it for?"

"I'm not sure," he admitted. "I have no fucking clue what I'm doing." He paused. "But I think for once in my life, that may be a good thing."

He hopped off the bar stool and pulled out his cell phone—he'd actually brought it tonight. Mack was looking at him like he was crazy, and he probably was. But that didn't bother him. In fact, he felt better than he had ever since he and Sam came back from the snowmobile ride and he'd found himself doing exactly what Claire accused him of—picking a fight just to push Sam away.

Better, maybe, than he'd felt even before that. Ever since he got the first letter from Kane Enterprises on that heavy, embossed stationery. Who cared what anyone thought? Who cared what he'd said he had planned?

Before he could change his mind, he opened up his recent calls and dialed the first number that came up.

Chapter Nineteen

When Sam returned to her room at the Cascade and pulled out her phone, she felt different. The messages from work didn't bother her anymore. Nothing had come crashing down in her absence. Her dad liked to say that his job as the head of the company was to steer the ship, not to rig the sails and test the wind and check the course, and, and, and. But there was so much scrutiny when Sam had taken over that she hadn't felt she could plant her feet and let the ship go. She wondered, though, if she finally understood what he'd meant.

The company worked best without her overseeing every step—but there were some responsibilities that were hers and hers alone. She hadn't gotten Austin to sign, but she was done delaying the rest of the deal.

She called the Hendersons, catching them right before they left the office for the evening. When she told them she was ready with the final offer they'd been waiting for, Arthur Henderson expressed how glad he was to settle the deal.

"I appreciate your patience as we ironed out the last details," she said diplomatically.

I appreciate your patience while I was busy getting distracted by the hottest thing on two legs. That won't be a problem anymore.

But she certainly couldn't give any sign of what had caused the delay while she was up in Gold Mountain. She had to get her focus back. Business was her world, her life. Look at what happened when she tried to do anything else.

The Hendersons were ready to see her right away. She could practically see their itching fingers, pens in hands, so eager for her check that they couldn't sit still.

She packed and left the hotel quickly. She'd drive to the offices and be back in Seattle by nightfall. Sleep in her own bed with the view of the city calling her home. There was nothing for her here, no reason to stay anymore.

In the car she checked her phone, but there were no missed calls from Austin. She wondered why she even bothered looking.

She was going to have to forge ahead without him.

It went faster than she'd expected. The handshakes, the scratch of the pen across dotted lines. Sam's heart pounded, but her voice was calm, projecting the assurance everyone had come to expect from Kane Enterprises. When they finished, Arthur offered her a drink to celebrate, but Sam shook her head. She had to get on the road.

"To the future," he said as he walked her to her car.

"Yes, the future." Her mind was in a fog. "And to Gold Mountain."

Arthur beamed. Of course he was thrilled—he had millions coming his way. Did he care about the prospects for the ski place? Or did he just want to pay off his debts and retire someplace warm?

She drove away with none of the fanfare she'd imagined during those long days and nights at the office, on the phone, scheduling conference calls, driving to and from the Hendersons' office to figure out one last detail and make sure everything was going to work. She'd finalized the biggest part of the development and the one on which everything hinged. Yet she wasn't feeling celebratory today.

The sky was beginning to darken in that slow way the mountains had of sucking up all the light. The roads were windy and still. Sam gripped the steering wheel, the relaxation of the massage a distant memory. She didn't realize how tightly she'd been carrying herself until the phone rang and she jumped.

It was Steven.

She knew she should have called him ages ago to explain what was happening, but she hadn't been able to bear it. He'd be upset she hadn't even tried to get the land from Austin, and worried about what the board was going to do as a result. She hated putting him in that position.

But she was done avoiding her messes. She picked up the phone.

"Congratulations!" Steven cried before Sam could say hello.

"Wait. You already heard?" The Hendersons were supposed to wait for Sam's lawyers to get in touch—they'd have no reason to preemptively announce the sale. If they had someone on the board they'd been negotiating with other than Sam, she was going to be *pissed*.

"I just got the fax a few minutes ago," Steven said, oblivious to her concern. "I don't know what you said to convince him, but you were right. The Kane personal touch really does go a long way."

"But I have the papers here," she said, looking over at the folder in the seat next to her. "I said they didn't have to do anything, I'd get it to the lawyers myself."

"They?" Steven asked, confused. "Is Mr. Reede married and we didn't know it?"

Sam choked at the words "Reede" and "married" snuggled up to each other in the same sentence. But instead of driving off the road, she asked, calmly, what the hell Steven was talking about.

"The fax I just got from Mr. Reede agreeing to sell the acres we've asked for." He paused. "What are *you* talking about?"

"I just met with the Hendersons. I brought an updated blueprint, and they signed everything I asked for. Wait a second." What Steven was saying finally caught up to her. "You're telling me Austin signed?"

There was a long pause before Steven dared to say to his boss, "You're telling me you didn't know?"

"Steven, this can't happen," she said. "Tell him not to. Or—no, don't say anything." She tried to think quickly. "Tear up the fax. Don't let anyone countersign—at least not until I get there. Okay?"

"Okay," he said warily. "But—you just said the Hendersons signed."

"I know."

"So the Hendersons signed before you knew for sure that Mr. Reede was going to comply?"

"Don't ask me what happened up here."

He ignored her laugh. "Listen, Samantha, you need to use this to your advantage. Whatever happened doesn't matter. You got Mr. Reede to sign, and the Hendersons, and now everything is moving forward as planned."

He was right, technically. So why did she feel so bad?

"Honestly, I've been worried," Steven went on. "It's been a mess. I didn't hear back from you, and I tried, but I ran out of ways to stall. I'm so sorry, I should have intervened sooner. When they knew I didn't have any updates—"

"I'm not mad at you, Steven," Sam interrupted. "I put you in an impossible position, and I apologize for not being more available when I should have been. Just tell me what happened when I was away. I promise it won't lead to any problems for you."

"The board called a meeting. For tonight, when they figured you'd still be out of town."

"They're kicking me out," Sam said flatly.

"If I can get them this new information, I can buy you time to bring them back on your side."

"Don't worry about the meeting. Let me handle it."

"But—"

"You've done enough already. I think I know exactly who to call. Do you have any guesses about who's been agitating the most?"

"Jim was in here asking when you were coming back, who you were talking to, why it was taking so long—that sort of thing."

"That's what I expected. Trust me, I can make this work."

"You got Mr. Reede to cave," Steven said with obvious pride. "I'm pretty sure you can do anything."

His praise made tears smart behind her eyes. She got off the phone before she officially started to bawl.

But she didn't have time to dwell on it. Steven was right—she had to move fast.

"Jim Rutherford," he said after the first ring, as though he didn't have caller ID and couldn't see exactly who was calling.

But fine, she'd play along. "Jim, it's Samantha," she said.

"Samantha, hi. To what do I owe the pleasure?"

"I hear it's been an exciting time at the office without me. I thought you might be interested to know, however, that I finished the signing. It's done."

"Fantastic!" he said, and she wondered if he was genuinely excited or faking it to cover his ass.

"I'm about to send a memo to the rest of the office

announcing the completion," she went on. "But I wanted to call you first."

"Does Steven know? Are you on your way back?" He paused. "Why are you telling me this, exactly?"

It was true, Sam should have had Steven set up a meeting to let the team know it was done and plan what came next. But she had her reasons.

"I know the board has been agitated," she said. "Some people have questioned my decisions, both publicly and privately. I'm not going to call out anyone directly. There will be no repercussions for anything that's been said or acted upon until now. Consider it a transitionary grace period, in light of personal and professional upheavals.

"But I want you to know unequivocally that from here on out, there will be no more agitating behind my back. If there's a problem, you raise it through the proper channels. If we disagree, we'll work it out according to the company bylaws. I respect you, Jim, but now's the time to accept that this deal is moving forward, and I will not be sidelined by my own board.

"And there's something else," she added, before he could start to protest or get into a debate she wasn't going to have. "In addition to calling to let you know the deal went through, I also wanted to apologize."

There was a beat of silence before Jim said, "What?"

"I'm sorry for the way I treated you on the phone the other day. I shouldn't have called so abruptly. There was no need for me to be rude."

She let her words sink in. It was probably the first time he'd ever heard her say anything like that—the first time anyone in the entire company had heard such a thing. Samantha Kane, the wolf, the bitch, saying she was sorry.

When Jim spoke, he sounded subdued. "I really appreciate that, Samantha, and I'm sorry, too, for the way I behaved. But I understand where you were coming from. It was done, and you had to make that clear." He paused. "I think you should know, though. I had nothing to do with trying to kick you out."

"Oh?" she said in surprise.

"Come on, Samantha. We may have our differences, but I know solid work when I see it. It's Greg and his minions who saw your father's death as a chance to get themselves a larger piece of the pie. But you're respected around here, and you will be even more so once this news breaks. Greg and his crew will back down. This was a big deal we just signed. A *huge* deal. And you brought it through."

Sam hoped it was true. She hoped what she'd done would be enough to hold her own and get the development Gold Mountain should have.

"Don't be nervous," Jim said.

She smiled to herself. "Would you be surprised to know that it happens sometimes?"

"But it's all working out as we've planned."

"It's working out how I want it to," Sam said, wondering if Jim picked up on the distinction.

"Now that sounds more like the Kane I'm used to," he said.

"I've got to go." She checked her GPS for the turn.

"Are you finally coming back to Seattle? I can't believe you spent so long trapped up there."

"I'm on my way," she said. "I'll get there eventually."

"No one's going to show up at Greg's meeting tonight. I'll make sure of it. And once word spreads that the deal is going through, his backers will peter out anyway."

"Thanks, Jim," Sam said and hoped he was right. She might still have some unhappy employees once they saw exactly what she'd signed. But she'd deal with it later. Right now, there was one more thing she had to do.

When she got to the split for the highway that would shoot her straight down to Seattle, she turned left, away from the lights, and climbed up, up, and into the mountains again.

Chapter Twenty

It was late by the time Sam pulled into his driveway. His house was dark, smoke curling out of the chimney. She pictured him inside, sitting with Chloe, finishing a beer—having a perfectly fine time without her.

Maybe she shouldn't have come. There was nothing they had to cover that couldn't be done over email, handled by Steven and other intermediaries. They were over—he'd made that clear.

But there were some things, she'd realized, that were more important than her company, the development, her father's plans, her need to return from Gold Mountain with Austin Reede's signature to prove she'd done it, she was the boss, the one who got what she demanded every time.

Austin was more important than that. And his land, his home, his happiness. His life. She was here to keep him from making a huge mistake.

She was also here to offer him a proposal she hoped he'd at least consider—even if it meant helping her, and the Kanes.

He looked completely surprised when he answered the

door. His hair was disheveled, like he might have fallen asleep on the couch. Sam had to force herself not to stare at how good he looked sleepy and undone.

"Can I come in?" she asked.

"Sam." He hesitated, running a hand through his hair. "I gave you what you wanted. Maybe we should leave it at that."

He sounded so sad, Sam's heart broke all over again. Yes, he'd given her what she hadn't had the courage to ask for directly, in person, the way she'd originally planned. But even though she'd technically won, she felt like she'd lost everything.

"I can't," she said. "I know it'd be easier if I went back to Seattle and we never spoke again, but I can't let this go."

She stepped inside. The lights were dim, the fire flickering low in the fireplace. Chloe, curled in front of the warmth, glanced up, realized it was Sam, and tucked her head back down. The sight of her, peaceful and trusting, tugged at Sam's heart. Chloe didn't think of her as an interloper. She thought Sam belonged.

But Sam knew she didn't. Her cream blouse and black slacks had been appropriate for the meeting with the Hendersons but now screamed *outsider* in Austin's cozy home. She knew he saw it, too. How had she ever thought she could get away with not being Samantha E. Kane for even half a second, no matter how far she was from the skyscraper that bore her family's name?

But it was too late for second thoughts. She was here, the blueprints were rolled in her hand, and a brand-new deal was signed. *One shot to convince him*, she reminded herself. What would her father say?

But she couldn't ask herself that when what she was about to propose was nothing like the plan her father had. She was on her own now. She had been for the last three years, but it wasn't until she'd stood in that office shaking Arthur

Henderson's hand that she truly understood it. She was the CEO, the one in charge. It was up to her to show Austin her vision and hope he'd understand the possibility she was laying at his feet.

She turned to face him.

"I'm sorry," she said. "I know I don't have a right to barge in here. I certainly don't have the right to ask anything of you. So you don't have to forgive me. But I still have to say it. I'm sorry."

Austin's lips tightened. She couldn't read his expression. She'd expected him to be angry, maybe even refuse to see her. She hadn't expected this sadness, the pain in his voice when he said, "Were you never planning on telling me? Were you just going to leave without another word, whenever you decided to head back to work?"

Sam stepped toward him but stopped before getting too close. She wanted to tell him she'd never do that, she'd never abandon him the way he'd been by his parents, coaches—everyone who was supposed to care for him when he was young.

But of course she couldn't say that. Because wasn't that exactly what she'd intended to do? Maybe not in those terms, maybe not once she'd started to fall for him. But she couldn't say it had never crossed her mind.

"I don't know what I was going to do," she admitted. "Obviously this wasn't something I'd planned. I really, really wanted to tell you—but at a certain point, I didn't know how."

But wasn't that another lie? A thing she was supposed to say even though time and time again she'd gone out of her way to keep the truth from him? She'd been so sure she'd done the right thing, or the okay thing, or at least not the most horrible thing by not disclosing who she was and why she was there. But seeing the look in Austin's eyes and hearing the platitudes come out of her mouth…

"No." She shook her head. "You're right. I'm past pretending—at least with you. I didn't want to tell you. I was terrified you would find out. Because this time we've spent together, the way we are together—" She met his eyes. "I wanted you, Austin. Against my better judgment I wanted you, and I knew that if I told you who I was, you wouldn't want me back. You and your friends would sit around talking about how much you hated me, how you'd fight me at all costs, and I'd never have a chance."

He blinked. "A chance at what, Samantha?"

"Sam," she said. "Please. The people who know me call me Sam. It's only at work, in public, that I'm Samantha, and I don't want to be that with you. I wasn't making that up when I told you my name. It was the only name that fit from the moment I met you."

"Answer the question, Sam," he said, and she was so relieved to hear that word come out of his mouth, the same name he'd cried when he was inside her, the closest to her that anyone could be, that it didn't matter how distant his voice was, how closed off he was from her now.

The force of the memory made her body pulse. It wasn't fair how her heart could leap up on its own accord, oblivious to anything else. She had to remind herself to heel. This wasn't the time.

Yet desire was a wayward child, reaching up, yearning, unable to understand why it couldn't have what was right in front of it. What it so desperately craved.

"When I first met you, I'm pretty sure you knew exactly what I was looking for." Heat rose to her face, but she didn't stop talking. "You turned out to be more than a one-night thing, more than a pretty face and a few good laughs before I had to go. I know I blew it, Austin. I'm not going to pretend I don't realize that." She paused. "But I actually came here in person to show you something."

"The papers?" He pointed to the blueprints she'd brought in.

"I might have at one point expected to give you a sales pitch. But there's something else I want to share with you."

She unrolled the blueprints on the kitchen table, using water glasses to weigh down the sides. He stood next to her, looking over her shoulder. She brushed her fingertips over his where he rested his palm on the corner of the blueprints and pulled away quickly, embarrassed by her sudden lapse.

"What is this?" Austin asked, like he hadn't noticed her accidental brush even though she could tell by the strain in his voice that he had.

"These are the basic blueprints for the original Kane expansion."

"Okay."

"There's your house, the woods, and the boundaries for the proposed condo development."

He nodded, but he didn't really seem to look. Sam pulled out a second sheet, a transparency, and unfolded it over the first. "This is just a sketch. I did it in the Hendersons' offices, so it doesn't look like much. I'm not an architect, I just hire them." She tried to laugh at herself, but Austin's expression stayed blank. "Okay, too soon," she muttered. "But look, this is what I want to show you."

She was in business mode now, running through the plan she'd come up with just that evening. Not what she'd said to the Hendersons when she first pitched them about the sale, words written up and pored over by lawyers, developers, architects, planners until the sentences twisted and spun, turning meaningless in her mind. Not at all what she would have said had she ever had that official sit-down with Mr. Reede. These were words she'd come up with on the spot, when all of a sudden it had hit her what had to be done. These were words she meant.

This wasn't her father's vision anymore, but her project through and through. She'd picked it up when she became CEO three years ago, but she had the power to shape it any way she saw fit. It was a tremendous responsibility. She could fail completely and disgrace not only herself but her father's memory and the company name.

Or she could be the one to change everything for the good.

Sam pointed to the changes in the roads, the sections of land, the areas where Gold Mountain would expand. "I don't understand what I'm looking at," Austin said, running his finger south from the serpentine line Sam had drawn to represent the main road running up to the lodge. "This whole area where Pine Point is—why isn't there anything drawn over that?"

"Because that's going to be left as it is."

"That's where we went on the snowmobile," Austin reminded her.

"I know," she said softly. As if she could have forgotten how they'd stood just that morning looking over the world.

He drummed his fingers on the table. She recognized the gesture as a sign of the energy that came up inside him and needed somewhere to go. It made him ski, run, work himself ragged. She recognized it because it was the same force that kept her in the office, working, thinking, making things happen. Making plans real.

She willed him to understand what she was showing him. She begged him silently to say yes, even before she'd fully explained what she meant.

"The sale with the Hendersons is done, Austin," she said. "I finalized it today."

Beside her he seemed to deflate, his size and strength and fortitude unraveling before her eyes.

"But it's not the deal that was in the papers," she went

on. "It's not the deal that's on this blueprint." She pointed to the first sheet she'd unrolled, the one below the transparency she'd laid on top. Saying this out loud was making her legs shake. What the hell had she done?

Austin stared at her. "Are you telling me you bought all this land but aren't going to do the planned expansion?"

Sam pulled out two chairs from the table. "Sit," she said, as though it was for his benefit and not because she was afraid she was going to tumble right over. Austin seemed to waver for a moment, as though still unsure about being next to her, but in the end he did, looking the table, trying to make sense of what she'd put down.

"Kane Enterprises now owns over fifteen thousand acres in the Gold Mountain ski area," Sam explained. "The only areas that are larger in the state of Washington—and in most of the country—are government lands."

Austin let out a whistle. She thought he looked almost afraid of her then, fidgeting in his chair, not meeting her eyes. And she supposed he had good reason to be. The thought of what her company now owned made her a little afraid of herself.

"It's going to be the third-largest ski resort in the U.S.," Austin said quietly, parroting the stats that had been circulating around the state. "More than enough to keep up with Whistler. Dwarfing anything outside Utah and Colorado."

Sam nodded. "Exactly." She paused. And then, when she was finally ready, she said the words that had been drilling through her brain the entire drive to Austin's. "And I want you to help me do it right."

Austin's leg stopped jostling midair. "What are you talking about?"

"I once asked you what you'd do to this area if you had unlimited—or, okay, nearly unlimited—resources. If you had the backing of a company like Kane."

"That was just joking around," Austin said. "I didn't even know you were—"

"Serious," Sam interrupted, because she wanted him to know that she was. "I know, again, that it was wrong not to tell you. I understand if you feel like I took you for a ride. But you opened my eyes to everything around here, and when I asked if you had a plan, something you'd want to do, you didn't hesitate. You said yes, because as much as you love it here, you know you could do something with the infusion of money and resources the mountain is about to get. And you know what you're talking about. You've studied this, you have ideas for what would work best, what people here need."

Sam was getting excited now, her voice rising, the telltale spark she got when she grabbed hold of an idea and couldn't let it go. It didn't matter that Austin was looking at her like she was out of her mind. She knew she was right—she knew this could happen.

She also knew she didn't want to do it without him.

"I'm not talking about us," she continued. "I want to be clear I'm not asking anything from you, or expecting anything in return for what I'm offering. We have our differences. I've made my mistakes. I'm sorry for what I did, but now I'm asking that we put that behind us." She plowed through the speech, no matter that the words cut like daggers into her heart. "This isn't about what happens between us personally. This is purely business." She looked at him to make sure he understood.

"Okay," he said, taking it in. "If it's not about us, then what is it about?"

"I want you to be my business partner. I'm asking you to take the lead on this development plan."

"You're crazy," he said right away.

"No. I've thought about this, and I know it's the answer Gold Mountain needs, and Kane Enterprises, too. I'm still spearheading the project, but you'd be the consultant — not in an office in Seattle, but out here. Your hours, your goals. Name your price. I can pay you whatever you want."

Austin rolled his eyes. "This isn't about the money, Sam. I've already sold you what you wanted. You can't just buy me off."

"I'm not buying you off. I'm hiring you for your services. You're experienced, you're qualified, you'd be great for the team. It's not every day someone comes along and gives you free rein, along with whatever salary and benefits you're looking for. Think long and hard before you turn this down just because you're mad at me. We can leave our personal issues outside of this. You don't have to talk to me about anything beyond business. But I want you on board." She risked a grin. "And I should warn you, I have a habit of getting what I want."

Austin exhaled slowly. "I see that." But he didn't get up, or walk away, and he didn't demand that she leave. That at least was a promising start.

She walked him through the sketch again, pointing out her initial ideas and reminding him of the issues he'd brought up. When Sam handed Austin a pen, he uncapped it and immediately began sketching, laying out the crossroads for a new intersection south of the mountain slope. "I've always thought this is the kind of area that could have something," he said as he drew. "It's not going to bring the same kind of congestion as piling it all on the mountain road, and the flatlands will help contain the runoff." He paused. "At least I think. I'm not a builder."

"That's okay, we hire those. You come up with the vision, then consult with them about how to implement it. Same thing for the condo developers."

"You're serious about this," Austin said in wonder.

"Four-point-seven billion dollars, Austin. I may think

nothing of a two-hundred-dollar pair of gloves, but once we're talking that many zeroes, yeah. I'd say I'm serious."

"But here." He pointed to the place on the map where his house was.

"That's your land. Those are your woods."

"No," he said. "That's the woods I'm selling you."

"I already talked to Steven. He's not doing anything with the documents. We won't countersign."

"Don't be absurd."

"Austin, why would you sign such a thing? You don't want to sell. And I'm not going to ask you to."

"It doesn't matter," he said. "The money, the acres—take what you want. You should have what you need."

She frowned at him. "Don't tell me you did this because you gave up. Because I'm trying to tell you this whole development is going to be different than anything we'd talked about."

"I know," he said. "I hear you. But don't you get it? I'm not giving up anything."

Now she was confused. "Steven told me you agreed to sell the land. Did I misunderstand?"

"I did agree. I faxed him the paperwork this evening. I'll use Jesse and Sue's lawyer to finalize the deal. But I'm not giving up. I'm making a choice to do something important for you, Sam. Because you want this, you need it for your company, and I'm not going to stand in your way. You don't have to come back with a different plan or some crazy offer to consult. I just want you to be happy. Even if I can't have you."

This time she did rest her hand on his, feeling the strength of him before she pulled away.

"Steven called me when I was already on my way back from the Hendersons, heading over here to see you again," she said.

Austin looked confused. "You mean you wanted to see

me even when you still thought I wouldn't sell?"

"This isn't a ploy, Austin. I told you, we can develop Gold Mountain in a way that grows the ski resort, helps the town, and keeps more land intact. I know I'm supposed to tell you that you don't have to decide anything now, take some time to think on it, but I can't. Say yes, Austin. Tell me you'll do this with me."

She spoke with utter conviction, and yet she was still surprised when he looked her in the eyes and said, "Anything to make this development work is something I want to be involved in."

"Not just involved in but leading."

He looked down. "I'd have to get used to this whole you-in-a-suit thing." He gestured to her outfit.

She laughed. "This isn't even a suit."

"Whatever. It's not snow boots."

"You wouldn't be in the office—I give you special dispensation to wear whatever you want." She paused. "Especially if it's that tight racing suit."

Oops. She hadn't meant to blurt out that last part.

She thought he'd laugh, but instead his eyes narrowed. "Will everyone in the office be mad if you bring me in without consulting them? Do they even know you've changed all of this?" He fingered the transparency laid over the original blueprint.

"No, they don't know. No, they won't be happy. And no, I don't particularly care." Sam grinned.

"Yikes," he muttered.

"We can talk all we want about team building, but the truth is that this is a top-down company. And I'm at the top. I didn't necessarily want it, and when my father signed everything over to me before he died, I insisted I wasn't ready. I don't care what Samantha Kane said in interviews—the real me didn't want to be in charge. It felt like somebody else's role." She looked past Austin's shoulder, out the window where a light snow had started to fall, white flakes catching the porch light he had turned on. "I guess it felt like that was my father's job, taking care of everything."

She looked at him again. "But what I realized while I was here is that this is mine now, and I can shape it however I want. We don't have to do things the same way they've been done for generations. My father wanted this land, but he's not around anymore to dictate what we have to do with it. If people who work for Kane aren't happy with the changes, there are a lot of companies that will take them with this name on their résumé. But I'm trusting that there are going to be more people who want to see what we can do up here and will want to be part of the company that transforms this region for the right reasons, and in the right ways. I know, it sounds so idealistic." She waved a hand as though brushing away an objection, even though Austin hadn't said a thing.

But a weight was lifting that she hadn't even known she'd been carrying—the weight of being half herself, one part of her more fully Sam than she ever was in Seattle, but another part, a part that was just as important and true, locked behind the screen she'd put up for him.

Now she had a chance to tell him everything, to be fully present sitting in his kitchen with her whole life in his hands, and rather than be terrified like she'd been when she walked in, she felt almost glad. She only wished it hadn't taken her so long to get to this place with him, and that rather than yell and push each other away, they could have come to this honesty before everything went and crumbled in their hands.

"I'll tell you what," Austin said. "I'll do this on one condition."

"Anything," Sam said, and she meant it.

"I'm writing up a preliminary contract, and you have to accept it."

Her eyes narrowed. "Do I get to read it before I sign?"

He laughed. "Of course. But I'm naming my terms, and this time I'm really not going to budge."

"I told you," she said, "whatever you want."

"Paper?" he asked, but they couldn't find anything besides the blueprint, so reached for a napkin. He grabbed the pen they'd been using and turned his back to her.

"What are you doing?" Sam demanded, trying to see over his shoulder, but he pushed her back so she couldn't see.

He lifted the pen and paused. "How much did that six-pack cost that you brought over last night?"

"What?" Sam was completely confused. "I don't know. Seven ninety-nine?"

Austin scribbled something else down. When he finally handed the napkin to her, she burst out laughing. "You can't be serious."

"Sign."

The laughter died in Sam's throat. His jaw was hard, his green eyes flashing. She knew this wasn't a joke. "This isn't legally binding, you know."

"I don't care. It's binding to you, and I know you'll honor it."

Sam shook her head. "I can't."

"This is the only way you'll get me."

"But it doesn't have to be this way."

"It does for me. Come on. Just sign."

Sam didn't want to, but she'd told him he could have anything, and if this was what he wanted, then he was right. She had to do as he asked. She picked up the pen and signed her name—her full name—the pen bleeding across the line he'd drawn below where he'd scratched his demands:

I, Austin Reede, do hereby agree to work as a consultant for Kane Enterprises for the annual fee of $7.99, plus tax.

Then he, too, signed and dated the napkin and handed it

to her. "For your lawyers, so they know what to write up for you."

Sam smiled. "I'll remember to make sure they don't overstep and try to give you some kind of salary."

"I told you," Austin said. "I don't want the work part getting mixed up with us."

"But there doesn't have to be an—"

Austin's lips were on hers before she could finish saying the words they both knew she hadn't meant. For a moment she was too stunned to respond, and then instinct took over. Whatever had been rising within her, leaping up as soon as she saw him again, extended its hands and warmed her from the inside out. Her lips parted and her tongue moved with his, tasting his sweetness, her hands reaching for him as he, too, inched his body closer, one hand brushing the hair from her shoulder and clasping her firmly around the neck.

"Not idealistic," he whispered, his forehead bent to hers.

"What?" she murmured, forgetting what she'd just said.

"You're not idealistic. Why can't we think of it as realistic? As something we're really going to do."

Slowly Sam pulled away. The kiss lingered on her lips, but his words brought her back to reality. To all she couldn't have. "We *are* going to do it, Austin. I know we are. But this has to be business, Austin. I can't—" She swallowed hard. "I can't do this again."

Austin reached for her before she could back away. "Sam," he said. "Please, listen to me. I'm so sorry for the things I said to you. I was angry for no reason. You didn't do anything wrong when I pushed you away."

She pulled back her hand. "Don't say that just to kiss me."

"No. I mean it. Please, let me have one more chance with you. You were kind, and generous, and cared about me, and I couldn't believe all of that was true. I thought I wasn't good enough for you. I thought if I let you in, you'd find some way to hurt me."

"You could have told me what happened to you," Sam said. "You could have told me about the gloves, your injury. Or you could have just said thank you. You didn't have to use them. You could have returned them on your own, or told me they weren't for you but done so without blowing up at me over things I had no way of knowing."

"You're right. I wanted to tell you everything. Desperately. But that scared me. Usually I keep that secret buried so deep nobody has any idea there's anything there. Everything is different with you, Sam. I couldn't keep that secret anymore and I just—"

"Exploded?" Sam offered when he couldn't think of the word.

He shook his head sadly. "It all came out so wrong. I let you in and I pushed you out at the same time. But I don't want to carry so much bottled up inside me. I want us to be able to talk to each other, be open when we need to. If we're going to be working together, we have to be able to trust each other. Both of us. No secrets anymore."

Sam pressed her body close to his, feeling the muscles of his chest, the solidity of him so close she wanted to lay her head against his heart and feel it beating.

"In the spirit of honesty, I think I may have lied to you again," she murmured, tracing her fingertips along his cheek, his jaw, over the tickle of blond hair on his chin.

He pulled away sharply. "What are you talking about?"

She rested her fingers on his lips, feeling the curve as though it were all new to her. As though this were, once again, the first time. "I told myself I came here for business reasons only. I promised myself—and you—that was it. But I can't pretend that's the only reason I came back."

Austin ran a hand through her hair. "I can understand if you want to keep this a working relationship. We might not be good together as a couple. I don't know. The best I can promise is that I'll try. But I don't want to mess anything up for you. I know you have a lot riding on this deal."

"No." Sam shook her head. "No, no, no."

"I'm just saying. I'll do the consulting even if that's all you want. I don't want you to feel like you have to do anything else just to get me on board. Because I already am."

Sam clasped her hand over his where he was touching her neck. She pressed him close to her, as though reassuring herself that he meant what he said. "One thing you can always trust about me," she said. "You know that if I'm doing something, it's because I want to." She paused. "But, Austin, you get to decide what you want, too. The job is yours no matter what happens between us."

"I want to do more than spend all my time skiing. Maybe my life can be a little bigger than home, the mountain, Mack Daddy's, rinse and repeat. Maybe I can have more of an impact this way." He paused and flicked the opening where her blouse collected in a vee down her chest. "But I don't just want to work for you. I don't want that to be all that we have."

"I'd still be your boss," Sam murmured.

He unbuttoned the top button and pulled down the fabric so the lace of her peach bra peeked through. "I think I can get into that." His fingers traced her nipples through the fabric. "There's one more thing we have to square away, though, if we're going into business together."

"What's that?" Sam asked, trying to keep her breath steady as her nipples strained, knowing he was watching her, teasing her, seeing how far he could push before her poise broke.

"We're starting off on uneven footing. I owe you something from earlier."

Another button gone. Still Sam trembled. "You don't owe me anything."

"Yes." The next button gone. Her breasts spilled out of the shirt, only one button at the bottom keeping it draped partway over her shoulders. "I promised you something this morning, and I didn't deliver."

Sam racked her brain. The whole day had been so long, she had no idea what he was talking about. "Let's consider it a fresh start," she said. "As long as we're honest with each other from here on out."

"I agree. But that's not what I'm talking about." The last button. He slid the blouse over her shoulders. It was luxurious, the brush of silk down her arms, the trace of his fingertips bringing goose bumps to her skin. Austin stepped close to her, enveloping her in his warmth. His hands slid around and cupped her ass through her pants.

"I was negligent this morning." He bit gently on her earlobe. How could it be this easy for Sam to sink into him? How could it feel this right to stand half undressed before him when just that afternoon she'd thought her heart had shattered?

"Stop thinking," Austin whispered. "I can hear you thinking."

"I don't understand how we got here," Sam murmured into his chest.

"Don't question—at least not until I even the score."

"It's not a competition."

"No. But you should know that I'm a thorough and dedicated employee."

He unbuttoned the top of her pants and slid his hand down the front, cupping her, letting out a grunt of pleasure as he felt her dampness through the fabric.

"You know I'd already write you a glowing review." She moaned as his fingers stroked her slowly.

"Ah, but my write-up on orgasms for the day would be an N for Needs Improvement, when I'll settle for nothing less than excellent."

Sam laughed. "What are you talking about?"

"On the snowmobile. You didn't get yours."

"Something tells me it'll even out over time."

"No," he said, biting the side of her neck. "I owe you one."

He turned her and lifted her up so she was sitting directly on top of the blueprints. She wrapped her legs around him as he worked his tongue down from her lips to her breasts. He reached around to unhook her bra and licked her breasts until her hips were bucking up into him, a direct line from her nipples down between her legs. God, she'd wanted this. All day she'd wanted this, primed by the morning on the mountain, desperate until she feared she would explode.

And then everything had gone wrong, but it wasn't wrong, not really—not if she could be arching her back on his kitchen table, her hips crinkling the blueprints she had worked so hard to produce.

His tongue trailed down her stomach, and he wiggled her out of her pants. "I've wanted to taste you all day," he moaned as he leaned her back and bit the tender flesh through her panties, then kissed around the inside of her thighs where fabric met skin. Sam moaned and pressed her hips up to him, begging him to take her without teasing.

He slid her panties down so she was naked on top of the blueprints, hot and wet and wanting. Then he knelt on the floor and circled his tongue over her clit so that her hips jerked and she let out a gasp. Her hands reached down and clutched his wrists where he held open her thighs, pinning her in place against his tongue. There was a time for foreplay, for buildup, but this wasn't it. Austin was entirely focused on making her come.

And he was going to. His tongue flicked and circled and danced until Sam was clinging to him, crying out loud. She pressed to his tongue as the wave built and built, and then it all came crashing down. She was wet all over the blueprints, wet all over his face, naked and panting while he didn't have a single piece of clothing removed. When he stood up, wiping his mouth with a sly little grin, she hooked her heels around his legs and pulled him down until he was lying on top of her, his jeans scratching her thighs as he pressed into her, hard and straining against his fly.

"That was dirty," Sam whispered as she wrapped her legs around him and ran her fingers through his hair.

"Hope you didn't care too much about these blueprints."

"I'll have to make another copy now."

"Don't want anyone at work to know what you've really been up to."

"Mmm." Sam squirmed with pleasure against him. "Sometimes it's okay to have secrets. Especially when they're this good."

He lifted off her. "Tell me you're not going back to Seattle tonight. Tell me you're going to stay."

She sighed. "I have to be in the office tomorrow. I probably have about eight thousand messages about the deal. It's going to be worse once someone actually bothers to glance at the contract and realizes how much of the specifics I crossed out." But then she looked at him, and she couldn't think about business anymore. "I do still have a toothbrush here, though."

He grinned. "Stay, then, and leave first thing in the morning." He ran his hand along her side, over her hip.

"You know, I used to think I wouldn't need to do that much myself up here once the deal was signed," she said.

"And now?" he asked.

Sam propped herself up so she was pushing him back, sitting with her legs wrapped around his waist as he stood before the table. She slid down so she was standing, naked against his clothes. She hooked her fingers through his belt loops and pressed her lips to his forehead. For the rest of her life, she wanted to be the one to kiss those worry lines away.

"And now," she whispered, "I suddenly find myself with a very good reason to stay."

"What reason is that?" he asked, so quietly she had to strain against him to hear.

She might have felt like she should wait, it was too soon, too scary, too big to jump in. But she was done waiting, pretending she was protecting her heart and sealing it off instead. "I went and fell in love with you."

Austin didn't just kiss her. He told her in every way—with his words, his tongue, his hands, his heart—that he loved her, too.

And then he led her to his bedroom, although she was tugging down his jeans before they made it to the top of the stairs. Yes, there was the project keeping her here. But more than that, there was Austin. There was the love they had. Wasn't that more than reason enough to do something crazy, something different, something to completely change their lives?

Austin seemed like he had his routines. Sam did, too. She wasn't sure what it would be like for either of them to make new habits, to open their lives in new ways.

But as he lifted her onto his bed and laid her back against the pillows, she couldn't wait to find out.

Epilogue

Sam flew down the mountain, wind on her cheeks, bright sun glinting off the snow. Austin was ahead of her, but she was close on his heels. She'd been traveling back and forth between Seattle and Gold Mountain for almost a year now, and all the skiing she'd done last winter had stayed in her bones. Although she still got a secret thrill in her stomach whenever she stood on the lip of Diamond Bowl and looked down, it was a surge of happiness that hit her—not fear.

Okay, maybe a little bit of fear. It was still a long way down.

But she liked the rush. She didn't think she'd ever stop being awed by this landscape—or the man she was with. She took the moguls with everything she had, bringing her whole body into each turn. Ahead of her Austin pulled up short, laughing, and she nearly bowled into him, spraying him with snow as punishment for beating her yet again.

It wasn't really a competition. They were out here to have fun, taking in an early-morning run before the rest of the town woke up. After a sweet, lazy summer in which Austin spent most of his time in Seattle, Sam had been sure to be in the mountains so he could take advantage of the first major snowfall of the year.

"Still remember how to do this?" he asked, breathing hard.

"Please," she scoffed. "I nearly had your ass on that run." She smacked his butt. Instantly he pounced on her, toppling her backward into a mogul powdery with fresh snow.

"Get off!" she cried, hysterical with laughter, but he pinned her there as her skis swung in the air. Even through their layers, lying in the snow, the weight of his body against her felt like home, felt exactly where her body belonged.

"Are you ready for today?" he asked, still not getting off her.

"Of course I am."

"It's a big day."

"It'll be fine."

"New Kane offices opening in Gold Mountain."

"It's not a big deal," she reiterated. "It's just so we can have a home base up here while the development is happening."

"Yeah, because the boss lady spends so much time at some guy's house in the woods. She's not in Seattle enough to get anything done."

"Or it's so we can actually be part of the town and not just come in when we need something. And the boss lady spent plenty of time in Seattle, so much that she was afraid her boyfriend was going to get sick of it."

"I'm more worried you're going to get sick of being up here."

Sam shifted under him so she could raise her goggles. She squinted, trying to read his expression. She'd thought they were joking, but Austin looked serious. "I'm never getting sick of you," she said. "Don't you know by now you're stuck with me?"

"Do you mean that?" he asked.

"I love you."

He kissed the tip of her nose. "I love you, too."

"So no more nonsense about me not wanting to be at your house."

"Well, actually." He took a deep breath. "I was thinking that if you're going to be spending so much time here, maybe it shouldn't be my house anymore. Maybe it should be ours."

He lifted off her and popped out of his skis. Then he knelt down in the snow. Sam sat up, brushing snow from her jacket. Was he saying what she thought he was?

Austin took off his gloves, the leather dark and warm. She remembered the first time he'd worn them, after she'd come back from the Hendersons' and spent the night at his place. They'd spent so long in bed they were scrambling by the time they had to leave, rushing to their cars. When Sam saw Austin reach for the gloves by the door, she offered to take them back to the store on her way out.

But Austin said no. "It's cold out today. I was thinking I'd take them for a test run. Leave those crappy duct-taped things at home."

Sam came over to him and took his hands in hers. "Your gloves aren't crappy. I know they mean something, and I wasn't trying to take that away."

He shook his head. "I don't need to hold on so much to the things that hurt me. It might be time for me to try something else."

Sam scrunched up her face, confused. "But I thought you said they reminded you of your uncle. Of good things—of someone who cared."

"Sure. But having only one thing like that—it also keeps present in my mind how little else I had. It's like I'm always carrying around the fact that I chose to shatter my knee instead of make the team."

Sam pulled down his hat so it better covered his ears. "You were protecting your mother."

"I don't know if I was saving myself or throwing everything away." His voice was quiet. They were on their way out—it wasn't the time to talk. And yet, in a way, that was the beginning of things for them, the moment their relationship became real. They knew they could say what they were thinking, whether it was the right time or not.

"It's okay to move on," Sam said. "It doesn't mean you have to give anything up. It's like you said when I fell on the moguls. It means you're learning, pushing yourself, trying something new."

"I'll move on if you stick around," Austin had said.

And now he was saying it again, only it wasn't just words anymore. He pulled a small black box from his pocket. Sam took off her helmet and dropped it in the snow. She couldn't believe she was being proposed to in the middle of a ski trail, her hair a mess, cheeks flushed, a trickle of snow melting down her cheek.

But of course this was how she wanted it, outside on a bright blue day, her heart pounding and so full she thought she might burst.

"You're smiling like a maniac and I haven't even shown you what's inside," Austin said, and she laughed.

"As if that makes a difference to my answer." But of course the ring was beautiful—he'd picked it out with help from Claire and Mack.

"Mack doesn't seem like the wedding ring type," Sam joked as she slid on the ring, glittering as brightly as the snow in the sun.

Austin laughed. "And yet she kept insisting she knew what you'd like."

"She was right," Sam said, and she meant it. "We need to set her up with Connor, finally get the two of them happy."

Austin's eyes bugged out. Sam hadn't meant to spend the moment talking about their friends, but she couldn't help it. Seeing Austin's expression, she laughed. "You don't think so?"

"You obviously haven't seen them *really* go at it." He shuddered. "It's not pretty."

Sam shrugged. "Sometimes the people you disagree with the most passionately are the ones you feel most passionately about."

"In our case, we worked out our differences. The two of them? I could never see it happening." He leaned forward and took her in his arms. "So, boss lady. What do you say? Are you going to marry me and ski with me until I'm old and decrepit and can't walk anymore?"

Sam extended her hand, warm from her gloves. His fingers enveloped hers, and just that brush with his skin made her crave his touch, his lips, his tongue. She pulled him toward her and kissed him, tasting him slowly, savoring. Enjoying everything she had.

When she could finally pull away, she brushed her lips to his ear. Still holding him, she whispered, "You, my love, have got yourself a deal."

They skied down and went home, fed Chloe, and sat drinking coffee at the kitchen table, talking about the future, their plans, the life they were going to build. Framed on the wall was a napkin stained with ink and two signatures, the promise that Austin would work for Kane Enterprises for a whopping $7.99. It always made Sam smile. *He* made Sam smile.

"Ready for practice today?" she asked as he reluctantly got up to gather his things.

"I wish I didn't have to go, but I've got to meet the new team. It's going to be different without Amelia this year."

"You'll have plenty of new talent," she said. "Besides, now you can say you coached the woman who's currently crushing it on the U.S. Ski Team."

"That *is* a plus." He grinned. "And she says she's loving it, which makes it even better. What are you going to do? Head to the office?"

"Hell, no," she said and laughed at his surprise. "I've got a million people to call. Starting with my mom." She admired the ring again. "We'll call your mom, too, when you get back. Okay?"

"Okay," he agreed, and she was glad he'd taken that step. She wished her dad were here to celebrate with them, to walk her down the aisle and give her stern, fatherly advice when she wasn't asking for it…but she knew he'd be happy with her choices, and proud of the way the new development was shaking out.

She might not have done everything right, but when she looked at Austin, his grin as he gave her one last kiss before grabbing his jacket and keys, she knew that whatever mistakes she made, she'd continue to work through. With a strong, loving man by her side.

Acknowledgments

Thank you so much to my dream team: Andrea Somberg, Alycia Tornetta, Kaitlyn Osborn, Nancy Berland, Kim Miller, and everyone at Entangled, who love the men of Gold Mountain as much as I do and have made this book the best it can be.

Nora Metzger and Trish Hayes introduced me to the beauty of the Pacific Northwest and provided invaluable feedback on earlier drafts, helping me figure out who Austin is and what makes him tick. Thank you also to Alison B. for her eagle eye, and to Nora for the important reminder, when I was worried Sam might be getting too much action, that there's no such thing as too much oral sex. Wise, wise words.

I'm lucky to have a travel buddy, Robert, who first went hiking with me in the North Cascades and helped me plot and draft and dream out loud as we were walking through wildflowers and snowfields in the sun. As I write these acknowledgments, he's bringing me a beer in Vermont after a day of kayaking and we're deciding what mountain to climb tomorrow. I can't wait to see what books are going to come out of this latest adventure. Thank you for being on this journey with me.

The person I want to thank most is you, the reader. I'll keep writing even if no one keeps reading. But it's so much better knowing you're here.

About the Author

Rebecca Brooks lives in New York City in an apartment filled with books. She received a PhD in English but decided it was more fun to write books than write about them. She has backpacked alone through India and Brazil, traveled by cargo boat down the Amazon River, climbed Mt. Kilimanjaro, explored ice caves in Peru, trekked to the source of the Ganges, and sunbathed in Burma, but she always likes coming home to a cold beer and her hot husband in the Bronx.

Sign up for Rebecca's newsletter at www.rebeccabrooksromance.com/newsletter to get a monthly email about Rebecca's adventures. And don't miss *Make Me Beg*, Connor and Mack's story and book two in the Men of Gold Mountain series, coming 2017!

Rebecca's website: www.rebeccabrooksromance.com
Twitter: www.twitter.com/BeccaBooks
Facebook: www.facebook.com/rebeccabrooksromance
Instagram: www.instagram/com/rebeccabrooksromance

His Best Mistake

a *Shillings Agency* novel by Diane Alberts

One night with a stranger... Security expert Mark Matthews has loved, and lost, and has no intention of ever loving again—especially not a woman who thrives on her life being in danger. Now, hot, meaningless sex with strangers he had no intention of ever seeing again? That's a whole other story. And it's all life as a single father allows him to enjoy. But when he meets Daisy O'Rourke, the game is on, because she's everything he swore to stay away from. She has bad idea written all over her, but he's in too deep to walk away now...

Worked Up

a *Made in Jersey* novel by Tessa Bailey

Factory mechanic Duke Crawford just wants to watch SportsCenter in peace. Unfortunately, living with four divorcee sisters doesn't provide much silence, nor does it change his stance on relationships. But when fellow commitment-phobe Samantha Waverly stumbles into his life, he can't deny his protective instincts. The only way out of her family dilemma is to marry Duke—for show, of course. The blistering attraction between them might be hot enough to burn down the world, but their marriage isn't real...or is it?

Also by Rebecca Brooks...

HOW TO FALL

Made in the USA
Lexington, KY
05 April 2017